SAVING ART

By
Douglas Tennant

Chapter One

        Art Jankowski was probably the most decorated
police officer to ever have served on the Morningwood
Police Department. He had dedicated twenty-five
years of his life to the service of the good people there
in Morningwood, Mississippi. No one could even
fathom the number of individuals that he had
impacted in one way or another over the years; and
now it was Art that so desperately needed someone's
help. Not just anyone would do though; as Art had
been completely through his Department's
rehabilitative process, with little to show for his efforts.
Prior to the incident, anyone who knew him would
refer to him as a ball of fire. Many were the times
where he would be found working straight through for
over twenty-four hours, without even as much as a
break. While all the others were tiring out and barely
dragging along; Art just acted as if he was on uppers
and pulled the others along with him. The years had
taken their toll on many an officer; but Art came to
work each day like it was his first day on the job. In
fact it was almost sickening to others at the brink of
burnout. That was however, until the incident.
        Art had a partner like no other and the two of
them made the perfect team in the detective bureau.
Art would notice things at a crime scene that usually
went unseen by the other officers. While others over
looked the very minor details; he reveled in unwinding
the toughest crime scenes with his superior abilities of
deduction. Prior to joining the Police Department, Art
had moved there to Morningwood from Canada. His
father had been a Royal Canadian Mountie, assigned to
serve a fair sized community. In a lot of ways it was as

if they were on an island; with the nearest town over
two hundred miles away. Art had made a point of
telling everyone that the saying, "the Mounties always
get their man," originated in that very community.
Having only a limited number of suspects to deal with;
if one could read the scene and track a mouse across a
busy train station, then running down the guilty
individual was a given. Many were the times that Art
went with his father on those tracking expeditions and
little by little he became a better tracker than even his
father. We're actually not talking about tracking
someone across the vast wilderness; but rather
watching the floor at the local General Store for
shoeprints similar to those left at the crime scene.
Everyone at one time or another had to buy supplies;
where the wear patterns left by the various footwear
narrowed the individuals down rather quickly. Art
had even taken a job at the General Store; to where he
could help his father without causing anyone undue
concern. But enough about Art; it was his partner that
completed this wonderful team. This man could in
practically every case, tell you just who the guilty
individual was within thirty minutes of being at the
crime scene. He may not have a name for that
individual; but he knew if it was the jealous jilted lover
or just a blind date which had gone terribly wrong.
JW, as all called him for lack of knowing anything else,
could actually read people. This ability just came
natural for him; he could tell who was lying, who
wasn't telling the full truth, and just who had
something to hide. He never got into the details of the
crime scene like Art and that was what so perfectly
completed this pair. By the time that Art was through
with his thorough investigation of the crime scene; JW
had already practically made friends will all the ones
living within the entire neighborhood. These two men

would then bring what they had together and JW
usually told Art who the guilty party was. At that time
Art would tell JW just how the crime happened and
what evidence they had on the guilty individual.
When these two first teamed up there was no such
thing as DNA; but hairs, fingerprints and blood were
practically as good in those days. Over the years they
had fine tuned their abilities to the point that their case
closure was up to almost eighty percent. Most of the
other detectives didn't have much good to say about
Art or JW; as they struggled to even achieve a twenty
percent case closure rating. As the detective bureau
grew, the two men were asked to put on several
training schools. It was definitely their desire to pass
on some of their abilities to their fellow officers in the
surrounding areas. This too didn't set well with the
other detectives; as they saw it as one more way for
these two men to further rub their success in their
faces.

Then roughly three years ago, Art and JW went
to a crime scene just as usual and found that they had
fallen into a very deadly pattern. They were just
returning from another crime scene when they received
this call and it was already sweltering outside. Art
immediately started reading the scene even before he
reached the house. He was consumed with looking at
partial footprints leading across the front porch, from a
light shower earlier that same morning. At this same
time JW started right in canvassing the neighborhood.
It would seem that one of the neighbors had not seen
the woman today who lived in this particular house
and had something she so desperately needed to pass
on to her this very morning. Upon reaching the front
door, she found it slightly ajar and slowly pushed it
open. Almost instantly she was horrified to see her
good friend lying in a pool of blood. Without even

thinking she went back to her home to call this in to the police and was now standing in the front yard awaiting their arrival. What she couldn't know was that the killer had returned to retrieve crucial evidence while she was away from the house. Now with her pacing back and forth in the front yard, he was effectively trapped inside the house. He hoped that she would soon go back in, but instead saw the police coming up the street. Proceeding quickly to the back door, he noticed another police unit already rolling up to watch the back of the house. Upon Art and JW's arrival, the man had already found a hiding place inside the house. The officers at the scene informed Art that the scene was secure. Taking them at their word, Art started meticulously going through the scene; with an increasingly nervous killer secreted only a little ways away in one of the adjoining bedrooms. This man hoped that the officers would not come into that room; as it had not been part of the actual crime scene.

Art had now been deeply involved in his investigation for the better part of an hour and the man in the closet was getting ever more frantic. It was rather hot in that closet, there was no air movement, he was sweating profusely, and had been simply standing there this whole time. However, it was JW who first caught drift of the potential danger; as none of the neighbors recognized the car parked directly across the street from the crime scene. He quickly moved to assist his old friend; almost flying across the crime scene barrier placed out along the street. This definitely caught the attention of the two officers stationed there, as JW really seemed to be in a panic.

Then becoming very vocal, he started shouting out, "Arte, Arte, I have new information."

Art knew that anytime his partner called him Arte, it was to warn him of impending danger and he should be prepared for anything. JW was just hoping that whoever was in there would simply stay put. His shouting however had exactly the opposite effect on this man who was now frantic with fear and needing another fix in the worst way. At this point he broke from the closet and was shooting at anything he came across. Art had already drawn his 38 snub-nosed revolver and so had JW; but they were no match for the stolen 45 that the man was now wielding in full attack mode. The man emptied his clip, shooting both Art and JW down in the process; prior to exiting the house just to face two officers with fresh guns. Full emergency procedures were put into play for Art, but JW was pronounced there at the scene. The only good thing that came out of this entire situation was that there was no fast paced manhunt for the guilty individual or the resulting high dollar murder trial. In fact, the man hadn't even made it off the porch, with his now empty weapon clutched tightly in his hand.

Art had been hit three times and the resulting surgeries took the most of two weeks to complete. The worst of the three slugs had proceeded clean through his liver and spleen; causing this surgery to jump to the top of the list. The other surgeries were delayed until they were for sure that he would make it through this one first. Art had lost a lot of blood and the doctors, between themselves, were only giving him a fifty percent change of making it. This same bullet also clipped his back bone, but could have been a lot worse, if it had only been over by a half inch. A second slug hit him high and to the left side of his body. The third slug caught him in the right hip socket and they had to totally replace this hip and socket. Art was not even able to be present as the entire State Law Enforcement Community turned out to lay his dearest friend to rest with honors. At this point the doctors had Art so sedated that it was almost three days before he found out that his beloved partner was gone.

When the day finally rolled around to where they released Art from the hospital, approximately one month later, it was to an awaiting crowd of Morningwood's finest. The City Mayor was there and he presented Art with one more medal; this time for valor in the face of conflict. Art really didn't feel that he deserved this medal; as his inattention in this situation had caused the death of his best friend and beloved partner. There would never be another friend or partner such as JW and this loss was absolutely consuming Art. He had injuries that would take all of his efforts to get over and all he could think of was JW.

Art had married a true southern belle by the name of Sue Ann and her family was at the pinnacle of the socially elite there in Morningwood. By no means did his cop salary afford the mansion that they currently lived in. JW just loved visiting with Art and his wife on the weekends; as it made him feel as if he was actually part of the upper crust within this city. These weekends, when the weather allowed, were definitely reserved for friends, neighbors and partying. Art's wife had totally gone out of her way to make their home the perfect party place. Their huge six bedroom home was situated on two acres of land directly in the middle of Morningwood. Most of the land lay immediately behind the house and looked as much as if it was an ocean of perfectly manicured St. Augustine grass. There were fig trees, pecan trees, Magnolias, tall pines, and flowers everywhere. In the middle of this area were two huge gazebos, which served as sentinels to the entrance of the cooking area. JW and Art both reveled in their abilities to outdo each other with their cooking and the food they provided was simply scrumptious. Cold beer flowed like water

at these parties and that was the one thing that Art and
JW refused to provide. The various individuals,
showing up weekly for these regular feasts, knew that
beer was the one thing they could always bring
without asking and was always welcome. Everyone
would start showing up at about five on Friday
evening and many were still visiting at about one in
the morning when Art and JW would call it a night.
JW was always allowed to stay the night on weekends
and it was as if he was a member of the family.
Located on the back of the property was a small
apartment; along with an ice room, laundry room,
shower and bathroom. The family's staff used these
facilities daily in the process of working there and the
bathroom was used heavily during these parties. JW
had practically homesteaded that tiny apartment and
as such was always ready for the weekends. These two
men weren't just partners, but practically thought of
each other as brothers. Art's wife had tried
unsuccessfully many times to connect JW with one of
her girl friends. However, JW just wasn't the marrying
type. He had even dated one of Sue Ann's closest
friends for well over two years, but she just couldn't
get him to the altar.

After leaving the hospital, Art wouldn't allow
his wife to take him home; as he just had to go see his
best friend JW. The cemetery there in Morningwood
was very green and beautifully manicured. JW's grave
had already been leveled off and grass had been rolled
out over the area of the grave. A rose bush had been
planted at the side of the head stone and no one would
even know that someone had recently been laid to rest
there. Art was not able to get around at this point and
only cried from his seat in the car. Sue Ann heard him
say several times that he was sorry and she just chose
to stay very quiet. Only Art and JW truly knew what

went on in that house on that fateful day. Upon
arriving home, several of their friends were there and
as usual it had turned into a full fledged party. Art
was helped into a wheelchair and Sue Ann wheeled
him out to where everyone was gathered. He was on
several medications and the doctor had strictly told
him that he couldn't have any alcohol. It wasn't very
long at all, while watching all the others having a good
time, before he told Sue Ann that he was tired. In fact,
as the weeks past, Art used this same excuse for not
joining the others many times over. He was consumed
with grief and was without a doubt one of the worst
patients that ever existed. Sue Ann hired him a
personal trainer just so he could get back on his feet,
but he totally refused to even try. It was just as if his
usefulness in this world had come to an end and he
had no further purpose in this life.

If everything wasn't bad enough, Sue Ann's
father died and the usual pack of vultures started
circling for everything that they could get. At the
probate everyone was in for a real shocker; as he in his
will had turned his entire business over to his
employees. His family's only stake was as a very
minor stock holder and none of these shares were in
Sue Ann's name. He hadn't left his wife penniless; but
with the immense debt that he had recently acquired,
they were no longer among the richest families in
Morningwood. Sue Ann had spent her father's money
like there was no end and now she was almost out in
the cold. Their beautiful home was paid for; but the
costs of the servants, insurance, taxes, and up-keep was
way more than they could now afford. They were
forced to sell their beautiful home and had to face the
fact that they had to down size dramatically. Art now
realized that he had to pull it together and do
something at least; as his wife really needed him once

again. They settled into a suitable three bedroom home in one of the more desirable suburbs; which was still much smaller than what they were once accustomed. Art reluctantly agreed at this time to start his therapy and finally went back to work using a cane to slowly get around. They set him up with the Departments rehabilitation process and he at least showed up for every session. This was not a quick process and lasted for the better part of a year. He was assigned to a desk during that time and was given the duty of looking over the other detective's case reports.

Most of the other officers may have only had a twenty percent case closure; but their success in court was severely hampered by their poor report writing skills. Art was given the duty of looking over their finished reports prior to them being filed. He saw glaring errors in each report; but his give-a-hoot had long since waned. Even when he returned reports for correction; the others knew that he really wasn't pouring his heart into this new job. He was only a mere shell of what the old Art had been and they all felt sorry for him.

Art and Sue Ann had only one child, a daughter Regina, who was aptly named after Sue Ann's mother. She in true silver spoon fashion had married while JW was still alive and her wedding was treated as the social event of the year by Sue Ann's father. Their family being at the pinnacle of the socially elite at that particular time, allowed Regina to marry a young doctor straight out of medical school. Everything couldn't have been grander; but even the shiniest thing tarnishes with time. The young couple hurried into having a child, bought the big expensive home and the young doctor entered into an established practice there in Morningwood. Just how many young doctors have looked back in perspective and have wondered just why they decided to go into medicine; which leaves absolutely no time at all for their family life. The young doctor did take Wednesdays off though; but that was for his personal time, you know, golf and such. One thing was absolutely for sure; the young doctor spent way more time with certain nurses than he ever did with his wife.

With everything totally falling in around them; Art and Sue Ann responded to a knock at the door. There they found Regina, standing with their five year old grandson in tow and dragging a suitcase. Everything was quiet for about a second and then the tears just started pouring. Sue Ann spent that evening discussing this entire matter with her daughter and the decision was made that she could move in with them for the time being. Actually this shouldn't have been much of a problem; as Art came home from work each day totally distraught and immediately started drowning his sorrows in beer. He had a favorite chair and never moved from that spot except to get another beer. Sue Ann would bring him his supper, but flat refused to get his beer for him. He no longer used a cane, but limped badly; as he more or less drug the hurt leg along, rather than using it. His going so long without therapy for his hip had left him in fairly bad shape. At this point Art could practically smell retirement and just wanted to get there so that Sue Ann would at least get his pension. His would be a rather good pension and even included medical insurance until age sixty-five. Art's whole purpose in life at this point centered on getting this for Sue Ann and nothing else seemed to matter. This attitude worried Sue Ann greatly; as it was as if he wasn't doing anything for himself. She talked with his Captain, but the Captain assured her that it would just take time for Art to get over what had happened to him. She told the Captain that Art had already dealt with what had happened to him; but would never get over the fact that he was at fault for JW's death. The Captain felt that this was absurd; as both men were doing everything they possibly could to stop that particular situation.

It was at this time, with Art overseeing everyone's reports, that the men started seriously rebelling against his second guessing them. Little by little Art had been trying to do a better job and the others just related this to his pushing their short comings into their faces. These men were very well aware that the Captain had received his chance years earlier at becoming a Lieutenant, simply due to Art passing it off to him. They definitely felt that Art was getting treated with greater favoritism than any of them and none cared in the least if it was due to the selfless act that he had shown years before. The Captain knew well that he was giving Art all the slack he could; because he felt that at this point Art would not be able to go back out on the street with another partner. That following week the Captain announced that they were creating a cold case detective position and it would go first to the detective with the greatest seniority. Of course this meant Art and he was not even for sure that he could handle this situation; so he asked to speak with the Captain in his office.

After a fair amount of whining on Art's part, about not being ready to go back out on the street, the Captain put it to him straight, "You either take this cold case position or it will go to the next in line. Then you will be assigned to work the street with that mans previous partner."

Art left out of the Captain's Office that day with his head abuzz and almost couldn't think about what all he would have to do. He called in sick that following day, which was Friday and thoroughly tried to drown his sorrows in beer all weekend. He didn't share this dilemma with his family; as he really didn't want their input on what he should be doing.

Art now had a five year old boy at home and was the only male in the house for this young man to learn from. The boat that was parked just behind the house was a tremendous fascination for this young lad and he wanted to know just why his grandfather couldn't take him out fishing. Even though Art knew that everyone in the house had to get along, he just couldn't handle the constant attention that this young man was giving him at this time. He didn't actually mean it when he jumped down the young boy's throat this one day and told him to go bother someone who cared. Teddy immediately went in to where the women were and repeated everything that his grandfather had told him. Sue Ann was fully prepared to go confront her husband; but Gina, as they all called her, stopped her mother. Gina said that their simply being there was a tremendous strain on her father, on top of everything else he was already going through.

Gina at this time came up with the idea of getting Teddy a puppy; just to keep him busy and out of everyone's hair.

Chapter Two

It was at this particular point where everything
started to change; as a mother Jack Russell Terrier had
recently given birth to a litter of five. The owners sold
these puppies on a regular basis out on the parking lot
of their local pet store. Gina and Teddy showed up at
the pet store and saw the people out on the parking lot
selling something; but didn't bother even checking into
what it was. They went on into the pet store and there
were several puppies available for them to consider.
Gina could see them leaving there with a Shih-Tzu,
Boston Terrier, Poodle, Yorkie or something of this
nature. Teddy just didn't like any of these and
centered in on a hound puppy. Nothing that Gina
could do would change his mind; so she just decided
that they would put this endeavor on hold, until a
more cooperative time. On their way back out to the
parking lot, they could now see that the people were
out there selling puppies. Teddy immediately wanted
to go see them and Gina just hoped that they weren't
hounds. It quickly became evident that the tiny
puppies were definitely not hounds; so Gina was
willing to look more closely at them. The sign read,
"Jack Russells," and fortunately Gina knew nothing of
this breed.
     As fate would have it, JW had passed from this
life; but could not take that final leap with his old
friend in such tremendous need. He had watched him
in the hospital, at his grave site, selling his beautiful
home, and then struggling to do absolutely nothing at
work. JW wanted so much to help his old friend and
prayed that he might somehow be able to help him
before leaving this world. Then all of a sudden he

found himself being born into a litter of Jack Russell puppies. He was thoroughly confused about his present state of affairs and couldn't see how this might possibly help his old friend. As the days past he wasn't getting any answers, but was sure having a lot of fun in this litter of five. The day that they were taken for sale, he was one very depressed puppy; as he just couldn't see this helping his old friend at all. One thing was for certain though; he was the only one of the puppies that had the mind of a fully mature person. He would sit and listen to the conversations of his owners and knew that they were about to be sold. It was just about this time that he saw Gina and everything started becoming perfectly clear to him. As Teddy leaned down to look more closely at the litter; he jumped up, sat up, rolled over, barked and ran around in a circle. This totally impressed Teddy and he instantly wanted this very smart puppy. Gina looked the tiny puppy over closely and decided that he was far more desirable than a hound. They paid the price and Gina insisted that they go back into the pet store. She just didn't want to show-up at the house without everything that they could possibly need to care for this puppy. On the way home she talked with Teddy and he assured her that he would keep his new puppy away from grandpa. JW was hearing all of this and just knew that he had to spend time with his old buddy Art. He wasn't quite for sure just how he was suppose to help Art, but knew that somehow the Lord had it all planned out.

Immediately upon arriving at home, Teddy just had to go in and show off his new puppy to his grandparents. Art took an immediate dislike for the small dog and wanted nothing to do with it at all.

Art said, "Oh great, now we'll have a dog lifting his leg all over everything."

JW heard this and was determined to show Art that he could be trusted in the house. This was a particularly tough duty for a puppy; as they usually just went right where they were at that time. He wasn't exactly for sure just how he was supposed to help Art, but at this point he wasn't even allowed near him. Teddy told his mother that he was going to call his new puppy Rex and JW totally refused to come to that name. As the months past everyone was getting fairly tired of constantly letting the dog outside. However, it was duly noted that Rex had not messed in the house even once. Art wasn't saying much, but he definitely approved. Sue Ann had asked Art if he would put a doggie door in and he totally shrugged it off; not wanting to be involved in this endeavor in any manner. JW had slipped in to where Art was on many occasions and would try to get as close to him as possible. On each of these occasions, Art rebuffed his attempts and rather vocally sent him out of the room. It thoroughly crushed JW seeing his old friend in this situation and there being absolutely nothing that he could do about it. There JW was the one who had died and he was feeling sorry for the ones that were alive.

As JW grew, so did his speed and desire to chase anything that moved. Sue Ann had a Turkish crystal hanging in her kitchen window. When the sun was on that side of the house, the small colorful lights danced all over the kitchen. Teddy would plead with his grandmother for her to move this crystal, to where the tiny spots of very colorful light would go everywhere. JW on the other hand practically went crazy chasing these allusive specks of light all over the kitchen, without ever catching one. Teddy, Gina, and Sue Ann would almost split a gut laughing at Rex's efforts in trying to catch the dancing lights. No matter how JW would try to ignore them, he just couldn't.

In years past, when they had the weekend parties, Art sure enjoyed watching the birds and squirrels that would venture near. Now he would sit out on the back porch and watch the various birds and squirrels that visited their new back yard. That was of course when the huge tomcat from next door wasn't out there scaring them all away. When JW first arrived, he ventured out into the back yard as an innocent puppy and ran directly into this very large tomcat. The cat quickly sized him up, circled him and informed him that he was the master of this yard. As JW slinked back towards the house, the cat told him not to forget this lesson if he knew what was good for him. Over this past year JW had gone clean out of his way to totally avoid this cat. However, he was now sitting out on the back porch with Art and sure enough there was the cat lying in wait for the squirrel. Art sicked him on the cat and JW knew that this was his chance to impress Art. No matter what might come of this, he just had to do it. Exploding from the porch as fast as he could possibly move; he quickly approached within five feet of the cat before starting to bark something fierce. It was this barking that the cat absolutely couldn't handle, as he went straight up into the air. When he hit the ground JW was nipping right at his tail. JW knew that he could have caught him, if he had just tried a little harder, but thought better of this situation. When the cat went over the fence, Art called the dog back over to where he was and patted him on the head. Art didn't like the name Rex and just referred to him as Dog. This was truly the first time that JW had been allowed to lie down near his old friend's chair. As he lay there, he wondered just what it was that he was suppose to do to help Art out of the slump he was in.

Art spoke-up, "Dog, you just need to keep an eye out, so that darn cat don't come back around." This was one thing that JW could actually do and possibly this was a start.

Gina had signed Teddy up to play T-ball, and Sue Ann had watched several of his T-ball matches with great enthusiasm. Sue Ann couldn't believe how Teddy had progressed and definitely wanted Art to come see what his grandson could do. Art had put her off on more than one occasion, but finally gave in to her continued insistence. The dog was not in any way considered part of their family; so JW usually got stuck in the back yard when they all went anywhere. Without a doggie door he would have no one to let him out and that first catastrophe might just happen. The T-ball match was held on one of the four baseball fields which were built back to back in a huge square. This was a very fine facility and had bleachers back to back for the opposing fields. Art and Sue Ann proceeded to a spot half way up the aluminum bleachers and she took hold of his hand as they watched the little ones attempt to hit the ball. It was a relatively pleasant evening, if you discounted the ever present and overwhelming humidity. Being from this area, they hardly even noticed that their clothes were also fairly well showing the signs of perspiration. They had been sitting there enjoying the little ones for almost an hour, when the world changed forever for Art. A fowl ball was hit high over the fence to their back and it came straight down into the bleachers, directly to where Art and Sue Ann were seated. People in the stands behind them were yelling for everyone to watch-out; but surely this was for the ones watching the other game. At this point the fast moving hardball struck Art in the back portion of his head, causing his whole body to lunge forward. It was just as if he had been shot all over again; as he tumbled forward into the people down below them. At the moment the ball hit Art, he saw an incredibly bright and very white light that simply dominated everything. While he was out, he was hearing all of what everyone was saying; but he just couldn't seem to respond in any manner. Finally the paramedics got him down out of the stands and onto a gurney. At this point he was still hearing everything that was being said, but still he just couldn't respond. On his way to the hospital he finally came around to where he could speak and was trying to tell them that he was alright. However, it was as if he was carrying on a conversation with no one else responding to what he was saying. They wrote down on their chart that he was delirious and convinced him to go on to the emergency room just to be checked out. Listening to what the paramedics had to say, the doctor felt as if he had suffered a slight concussion.

After being transferred to a hospital room, Art's family was finally allowed to come in and see him. Sue Ann came up to his side, put her hand on his and was just looking down at her husband once more lying there on a hospital bed. Art heard Sue Ann tell him that she was sorry for insisting that he come to that dumb T-ball match.

He told her, "You have nothing to be sorry for and I definitely don't feel that the T-ball match was dumb. In fact, I rather enjoyed myself."

The only problem with this was that Sue Ann had not said anything. She had only been thinking this as she came over, looked him in the face and took hold of his hand.

Sue Ann spoke-up, "I didn't think I had said anything, but I sure must have been thinking it out loud."

This really messed with Art and he didn't hear anything further until the doctor came in much later. The doctor was standing there as the nurse took his pulse and he heard the nurse say that the doctor probably would never leave his wife. Art had been watching the nurse and she hadn't actually said anything. He was now fairly well for sure that he had read her thoughts and it really messed with him a lot. Possibly when the swelling on his head went down, this would all blow over.

The following morning Sue Ann showed up at about nine in the morning. The doctor had been in to see Art earlier and felt that he was well enough at this point to go home. They wheeled him out of the Hospital and he felt like an invalid. It had been in this same manner that he had been wheeled out after being shot. He remembered that day well; as he almost couldn't get out of the wheel chair and into the waiting car. This time however, even though he had quit his therapy, he was fully able to at least stand and easily get over into the car. They were on their way home and everything was fairly quiet between the two of them. Art was purposely watching Sue Ann to see if she was saying anything. If she spoke, he for sure wanted to answer her. This ability of his to read thoughts was going to be difficult if it lasted for any time at all.

Then just as if she had spoken, he heard, "I wonder how long he will be off work this time?"

Art didn't want to make her aware that he had read her thoughts, so he started in, "How's everyone been doing?"

Sue Ann replied, "Everyone is doing just fine, but you should see what Teddy is doing with that dog of his. He somewhere came up with one of those red dot pointers and has Rex doing everything. It's absolutely hilarious."

"I'll bet so," Art replied. "I'll need something to do for the remainder of this week. The doctor wants me back in here in three days to see if he will release me to go back to work."

This answered Sue Ann's question without her even asking it. The remainder of the trip home he felt that Sue Ann must have not had any more thoughts; or possibly this thing, whatever it was, just happened to be wearing off. What he didn't know was that the person had to be touching him, or nearby personally thinking of him for Art to read their thoughts. Arriving home with Gina and Teddy there, the sounds and thoughts started pouring into his head. It was very evident that he was hearing and reading thoughts at about the same time; as he was having a hard time understanding just what was actually being said.

Finally Art just put his hands up in the air and said, "Please, just one at a time. I'm still trying to recover."

The women told Teddy to take his dog outside, Art got settled into his favorite chair and Gina brought him one of his favorite beverages.

He smiled and said, "Its sure good to be back at home. Gina wasn't giving off any thoughts about Art, so he wasn't picking up on anything. Her thoughts at this point were of Teddy and his dog.

"You really need to see what Teddy can do with his dog now, it's amazing. When you feel that you can handle them, I'll send them in."

Art knew that he needed to do this or be plagued with requests for the next several days, so he said, "By all means, send them in."

In short order Teddy and his dog graced Art's presence, and Teddy had brought his red dot pointer with him. Upon entering the room, he said, "Grandpa, watch this," as he turned the red dot on and started running the dog in circles. Then he started running the dot up the wall and the dog was jumping up and biting at the wall. Finally Teddy started running the dot back and forth and the dog was almost running over himself turning around.

It was at this time that Art thought he heard, "Art, please stop him, I can't help myself."

Art spoke up, "Teddy, why don't you give him a rest, you don't want to hurt him do you?"

Teddy just turned the pointer off and said, "It doesn't hurt him grandpa; he likes doing this."

Then Art thought he heard, "But let's just not get carried away, alright?"

This time he was watching Teddy and knew he had not spoken these words; just possibly the dog had thought this and he had read his mind. That was absolutely going too far. Art didn't want anything to do with reading some dog's mind; so he asked Teddy if he would go see if grandma would mind getting him another beer.

JW walked out of the room without even suspecting that Art had read his thoughts. In fact he had really started fitting in as the family dog; all the while waiting for some possible opportunity in the future to help his old friend.

Art stayed up watching TV late each night; as he basically had trouble sleeping. Whenever Teddy was fast asleep, JW would jump down and come in to where Art was sitting. Invariably he needed to go outside. He hated to put his old friend out; as he knew he basically didn't like being bothered by the dog, but there was no other choice. As usual, JW barked once by the back door but nothing happened. He then walked in and looked right at Art; who was evidently deeply involved in the movie he was watching.

The next thing Art thought he heard was, "Hey buddy, would you mind letting the dog out?"

Once more Art only laid this off as being part of his current medical condition and slowly started to get up out of his chair. He went to the back door, heard nothing further and let the dog out. This had practically become a nightly affair; so Art knew that the dog would just start barking and hitting on the back door if he didn't wait to let him back in. At this same time JW in consideration for his old friend, hurried his business along and didn't dally any longer than necessary. Art saw him coming across the back yard and pushed the door open just in time for the dog to shoot back in.

Art was tired, but clearly heard, "Thank you, I needed that," and responded, "Your welcome."

Now both the man and the dog were just standing there looking at one another in amazement.

Once more Art heard, "It sure sounded like you just told me that I was welcome."

Art slowly spoke-up, "Could you understand what I just said?"

JW was turning his head from side to side and thought, "Could you possibly have understood what I just thought?"

"Enough of this nonsense," Art said. "Go on, get on out of here."

The dog took back off in the direction of Teddy's room and Art went back to watching his movie. Later, as usual, Art had fallen asleep without even knowing how the movie ended. It was at this time that he was awakened by someone talking to him. He was slow to wake and started responding without even thinking.

The voice was saying, "Come on Art, wake up, its bedtime."

He replied back, "I'm up and I'll be right in there dear." However, when he looked around there was no one there except for the dog.

Then he heard, "You did read my thoughts didn't you?"

Looking right at the dog, Art said, "No I didn't read your thoughts and I'm not going to be accused of talking to a dog."

Starting for the door to his bedroom, he heard, "But it's me Arte, JW."

Arte was the word that JW used when people were around and he wanted to put Art on his guard. By the same token Art would call JW, Bill, if something didn't appear just right.

Stopping in his tracks; Art turned and looked right at the dog. "JW, is that you?"

"Yes, that's what I've been trying to tell you. For some unknown reason, possibly your grief, I was placed in the body of this dog to somehow help you."

Art just looked over at the pile of beer bottles, rubbed his head and said, "Wow, I'm having some seriously strange delusions."

Then from the other room a voice came, "Art dear, are you coming to bed?"

Art just waved his hand like waving this whole matter off and headed off for the bedroom. JW now knew that somehow Art could hear just what he was thinking, but how was he going to convince his old buddy of this. He thought about slipping into their bedroom and just continuing his conversation with Art; but he didn't want to see Sue Ann have him committed for talking to the dog.

Chapter Three

That next morning Art was able to sleep-in; as everyone else had somewhere they needed to be this day. After everyone was gone, JW eased into Art's room and hopped up gently on the bed next to him. Art was a light sleeper and felt the bed move. He rolled over just to be looking right at the dog.

Then Art heard, "Well you can't put it off as being tired or drunk this morning, and yes it's the dog that you are hearing."

Just lying there, Art was trying to make some sort of sense of this whole situation. He knew that he had been able to hear the thoughts of some of the individuals around him; but to hear the thoughts of a dog, let alone one that claimed to be his old partner, JW.

Art spoke-up, "Did I hear you right last night? Were you telling me that you were somehow JW, my old partner?"

The dog became fairly excited now and that just made everything worse, "Yes, that's exactly what I've been trying to tell you."

"Then tell me something that only JW and I would know," Art asked?

"How about that one time when we worked the death of that Pimp down on 5th Street and how we found him. He was sitting up in a chair, holding an open can of chili in one hand, and a bent nine of hearts card in the other, which he had evidently been using as a spoon. Oh yes, and then there was the pink dildo sticking down the back of his pants. We wondered where the strange noise was coming from, as it was still vibrating."

Rolling quickly out of bed, Art didn't know what to think of this; but knew that this just wasn't right. He hurried to the bathroom and quickly shut the door behind him.

This didn't do the trick though as he soon heard, "Well, wasn't I right."

"Go away;" said Art, "This just can't be happening."

He heard, "Well if it can't be happening, then why are you still talking to me, and just how did I end up in this dog's body anyway?"

Art wanted to get rid of the dog, so he said, "Cat, there's a cat in the back yard, go get him boy."

Then shortly he heard, "Good one Art; I was almost half way to the door when I remembered that you refused to put a doggie door in to where I could go out by myself."

Thinking about it for a minute, Art said, "If you can understand what I am saying, then I want my house slippers by the door when I come out."

Finishing his shaving; Art reached over to open the door, and there was the dog with his house slippers. He said, "Alright, I might be able to justify that this bump on my head is allowing me to read thoughts, but dog thoughts?"

"Well its happening somehow," JW thought.

"But how is it that you can understand just what I'm saying; that's not something that just comes natural for a dog."

He heard, "That's what I've been trying to tell you. I'm not a normal dog; I'm JW in this dog's body."

The next two hours were spent trying to prove that the dog could not understand English, with very little success. At one point Art had him reading the newspaper to him and Art was hearing every word that the dog thought as he read the paper. It was just

about this time that the family returned for a bite of
lunch.   Sue Ann was pleasantly surprised to find that
Art was out of his chair, not drinking as of yet, and had
been at least moving about the house. They drug the
ham out of the frig that Sue Ann had cooked yesterday,
and everyone settled in for another good meal. Gina
noticed that her father had slipped the dog a few bites
of ham and wondered just what had brought that
about. Up until now Art had been dead set against
anyone feeding the dog from the table. In fact he had
become rather vocal about this not happening in his
house. Gina didn't say anything at that time, but later
brought this to her mother's attention. Sue Ann had
also noticed what Art was doing, but just decided to
not say anything at this point. Art announced that he
was tired and was going to his favorite chair for a nap.
Sue Ann asked if he would like a beer and he politely
refused; as he said that he might be going out in a little
while. All this time Rex had been lying there next to
Art's chair and nothing was being said at all.

Sue Ann came in to where Gina was and said,
"Something's just not right about this; Art refused a
beer, said he might be going out and Rex is just lying
right there next to his chair."

"Possibly this time together has caused dad to
accept Rex at last," she replied.

The women left out once more and Art went
back to questioning the dog. There was the rock solid
fact that he could read the dogs thoughts and he would
even have to admit that the dog did understand
English; but his being JW would surely be a stretch of
anyone's imagination. Every time that Art asked him a
question, the dog had just the right answer. Art
couldn't get it out of his mind that he might in some
way be giving the dog the answers; as after all he too
knew these answers and would very much like for this

to be his old pal JW. After much discussion, it was actually the dog that came up with the irrefutable answer.

Art heard, "Would you do me a favor and see that the Probate Judge gets my Will?"

"What Will," Art asked, then he remembered, "You mean that goofy little hand written thing that you had me witness?"

"Yes that," JW thought, "I want the Probate Judge to know just what my wishes are."

"That scrap of paper is probably long gone by now; as they've cleaned-out all your things and there's nothing left."

Jumping up on Art, JW thought, "No, I put it in the safest place ever, on page one thousand of your dictionary. After all, you never use it."

Getting up out of his chair, Art said, "Come on Rex, let's go shopping."

He looked back and the dog was just sitting there. Then he heard, "I definitely do not like that name."

"Well we certainly can't call you JW or they'll definitely put both of us away," Art commented.

"Then how about Bill," JW thought?

Bill had been the alert signal Art had used when things just weren't right and it just seemed to fit this situation perfectly.

Art spoke-up, "Come on Bill, let's go shopping."

They both climbed into the car and took a short ride down to the home improvement center. Bill was right on Art's heals until they reached the entrance. Art reached down, picked Bill up and placed him in the basket. This was the first time that Art had actually held Bill and it made JW feel really good.

Then Art added, "No barking and no marking your territory."

Bill thought, "Remember, I should be smart enough to know better."

With a smile, Art only added, "Good."

The primary reason for coming to this store was the purchase of a doggie door for Bill. They jointly picked the door out, returned home, and were almost through installing it when the women and Teddy came home. To say the least, Sue Ann and Gina were both very surprised.

Gina even had the nerve to say, "I see that you and Rex are really hitting it off."

Her father came back, "He doesn't like being called Rex and wishes for everyone to call him Bill."

Momentarily this stunned everyone. Then Sue Ann started in, "Rex, come her boy, come here Rex," but nothing happened. Then she simply said, "Bill," and he instantly came to her. She remarked, "I don't even want to know how you learned that."

After the doggie door was properly christened; Art and Bill retired to Art's favorite chair. From that day forward Art would put the foot rest up on his recliner and that was where Bill could be found. Teddy would come in and want to do something with his dog and Art would suggest that they all take a walk. At first Art was rather slow, but in due time he picked up his pace considerably. Now the three of them were finally doing something together and this suited Sue Ann and Gina very well.

After this Bill and Art were inseparable and that also included the time they spent at work. Teddy was a little putout with this situation; but nothing that a couple of new video games wouldn't take his mind off of.

The first day that Art showed up at work with Bill, he knew there would be repercussions; so he went straight to the Captain's Office and lied. "Captain, it's like a miracle or something. My doctor and I talked about my problems and he came up with the idea of me using a dog as a substitute for JW. I've tried it and it's really been working out great for me."

The Captain was not one to go against doctors orders and anything that worked out for Art at this point was certainly welcome. Art only had three years left before he could get full retirement and the Captain was going to do everything in his power to make this happen. Sure enough, several of the others complained about not being able to bring their pets to work. However, the Captain stood fast and told them they could with a written note from their doctor. He never asked Art for a written note; as he could definitely see a marked change in him for the better.

That first day back at work, Art went straight to his dictionary and had no doubts to whether JW's Will would be there on page one thousand, just as he had been told. He looked at the hand written half page document and then at Bill.

"Are you for sure this is what you want? It leaves everything to your sister and totally denounces your brother."

He heard, "Yes, my brother deserves nothing except for denouncement."

With JW's Last Will and Testament in his hand; he lied once more and told the Captain that he just happened to come across it. The Captain noticed that Art had been the one to sign as witness to JW's signature and made sure that it got to the proper Probate Court.

The first order of business for Art and his new partner was for them to actually look through the cold cases that had already been assigned to Art. Up to this point Art had only looked at them and the papers might as well have been blank. With a fresh new perspective and Bill's insight, things quickly started coming to light, and questions started surfacing. On the very first case that they worked; there were several pieces of evidence that had been collected and a few had a rather strange odor to them. Bill convinced Art that they now had two additional crime solving tools at their disposal; that being his nose and his hearing. One thing they desperately needed was for Bill to know the distinct smell of the various drugs. Art called down and made an appointment with a drug enforcement property clerk, who just happened to owe him a huge favor. This man allowed them to come to the property room door; where he would read the analysis from the bag and Bill was allowed to simply sniff the evidence. No one but the clerk was allowed to touch anything and this maintained the proper chain of evidence. This worked very well at first; except that one particular batch of cocaine was not what was labeled on the analysis and Bill knew it. Art on the other hand knew that this was a very touchy situation; as he and Bill should not have been anywhere near this property and couldn't really say anything about what Bill knew. As they proceeded back to their office they discussed this situation at length; as it was bad enough just knowing about the discrepancy.

Back up at their office they went through the evidence collected on their first case and Bill decided that cocaine was the strange odor he smelled coming from the various items. Reading the cold case report once more, no one had mentioned anything about drugs at that time. Bill definitely thought that the various individuals might be more talkative after all these years. Besides, he had the body odors off of the evidence to work with now and needed to see who these particular items came in touch with. One of the greatest problems working cold cases was definitely finding the individuals who were even involved in past matters. Art being placed over the cold case investigations and not given a partner was also not assigned a departmental vehicle. When he needed to go anywhere, he was forced to go to the City Car Pool and check out a vehicle. This was the place where all the worn-out and wrecked vehicles found a last resting place; that was until they could go no further. It bothered Art to even be seen in one of these pieces of junk; but Bill was pleased with anything, as long as he could stick his head out the window. They had been searching for almost a week now, but could not come across even one of the individuals mentioned in the report. It was just as if they had totally disappeared.

It was now Friday evening and Art for the first time in a long time had put in an honest full weeks work. He was tired, but felt really good about what they had accomplished this week. Back at home everyone was amazed at how Art had taken to Bill and just how he had suddenly changed. The day that Art first took Bill to work with him; Sue Ann worried all day that she would receive a call asking her to come and get the dog, but it just didn't happen. Just as Art was about to settle in and enjoy his first beer of the week; a car pulled up out in front of their house.

Bill looked out the door and Art heard, "Oh no, that's my brother, what in the world does he want!"

Art quickly went to the door and met the man out on the sidewalk. Bill went with him and was definitely not holding his thoughts back.

JW's brother didn't stick a hand out to introduce himself, but rather started right in, "Did you actually witness James's hand written Will?"

"Yes I did," Art replied, "and I take it that you're the brother referred to in the Will."

"That's right, but that Will has messed everything up now; as James and I had settled our differences prior to his death."

The dog was going crazy at this point and Art had to tell him to get back. He was relaying to Art that his brother was lying through his teeth and that they had never settled anything.

Art said, "Well he didn't tell me anything about the two of you settling your differences; so I guess the Will is just going to have to speak for him."

"So you're planning on showing up to testify to its authenticity," the man remarked.

"I'm planning on being there for sure," Art replied.

The man aggressively stepped towards Art and said, "I would definitely change my plans if I were you. This just might not be good for your health."

Then Art heard, "Tell him that JW did tell you what he did and things are fixing to come to light. Tell him that he might even want to leave the country if he knows what's good for him."

Art didn't go into that much detail and just said, "Your brother did tell me what it was that you did and I'm looking into it."

If this man had been carrying a gun; Art felt that he would have pulled it at that very moment, but he wasn't. After he peeled away from the front of the house, Art asked, "Just what was it that your brother did anyway?"

Bill took off for the house and Art heard, "It's a long story and it may take a few beers to wash this one down."

Art let it drop for the time being; but after dinner they went out on the back porch where Bill started in, "There were three of us children growing up and father ran an incredibly profitable raw gem import

business. We lived in a rather large mansion and were
practically raised with the proverbial silver spoon in
our mouths. Eventually mother and father went their
separate ways; causing everything to be split-up in the
process. In the divorce father gave mother the
mansion; as her inheritance had paid for most of it. He
also had to sell off most of what they jointly owned in
the process of the settlement. Our mother was going
through some sort of mid-life crisis and told father that
he could have us children. She sold everything, moved
to France and we ceased to have any further contact
with her. Father did his best, but he was working
himself into an early grave. He tried everything he
could to put his now crippled business back on its feet.
The people around us thought that we were a bunch of
red neck hicks; as my father had named me James
William Aaron and my brother Joseph William Aaron.
However, he referred to us as Jim Bill and Joe Bill. My
sister was the only one who was referred to by what
we thought at that time was a normal name. She was
christened, Leander Belle Aaron, but father called her
Lea Belle. Our home was no longer a mansion and we
no longer had any hired help. Our manner of dress
was a bare minimum and our older sister, Lea Belle,
practically raised us boys. My brother and I left home
at the very first opportunity that we could. I lied and
went into the military while I was still only sixteen.
Whereas my brother never did anything with his life
and just run the streets, over in New Orleans I believe.
By the time that I was forty three years old, father died
and left his business to the three of us children. My
brother and I had never shown any interest in father's
business; but our sister had never married and had
worked side by side with him for all those years. For
this reason I felt that father's business rightfully should
have gone to her. I hate to say it, but by this time my

brother was thoroughly tied into drugs and crime. I just knew that I would hear one day that he had died some horrible death. Strange isn't it, the way that things actually worked out, with me being the one that's dead. Anyway, when I sided with my sister it left him no recourse and he refused to have anything further to do with either of us. It would seem as though, over these many years, my sister's business had become very prosperous. I simply couldn't bear the thought of father's business being butchered once more, just so that he could put more drugs into his worthless body. Then just about six years ago, he came to me demanding that I join with him and force our sister to buy our interest out. When I refused and told him to get away from me; he commented that a settlement would be far better than the two of us ending up dead. I told him that he didn't have the balls. He then broke it to me that I should ask the two dead robbers if he truly had the balls. I knew very well which case he was talking about and it had not been assigned to us. Detectives Thomas and Little were the ones assigned and I personally had no faith in their ability to solve that case. However, I did ask if they had any suspects. They just told me that it looked like a falling out between partners and they had no leads to the identity of the third man."

Chapter Four

At about this time, Bill changed thoughts, "Art, why in the world are you still carrying that wimpy little wheel gun. Didn't those just get both of us in serious trouble before?"

Art replied, "Well I guess that I should really look at something a little better; but I actually didn't think that I would ever have need for one again."

That's the exact same kind of thinking that got me killed. We need to go shopping tomorrow for a new pistol for you."

"Alright, but don't say anything to Sue Ann; because she really doesn't like guns and only tolerates the one I have to carry," he added.

Bill looked him right in the face and Art heard, "Yea, like I'm going to just run right in there and tell her. She probably wouldn't believe me anyway." With this they both got a good chuckle.

The two of them were now inseparable and Art had already started to explain to the individuals they came in contact with, that the dog was actually police issue. They proceeded down to the gun store the following morning and Bill promptly jumped right up on the glass counter containing the pistols. A man quickly headed over their direction and was about to say something; but Art pulled out his badge first. Nothing was actually said, but it was evident that the man just didn't feel comfortable with the dog up on his glass show cases.

Bill walked around and then barked, but Art heard, "Here we go; this is just what you need."

Heading over to where Bill was now pawing at the counter; sure enough it was the counter with the 45s in it.

The store owner commented, "You're dog seems to have a mighty fine sense for the better quality pistols."

Art remarked, "I don't know if I could handle one of these. Do they kick very much?"

The store owner remarked, "Smooth as silk. If you can handle that short nosed piece of nothing that you're carrying, with hot loads, then a 45 would be nothing. For the price of a box of shells you would be very welcome to try one of these out on our range."

Art was not so sure and felt that he surely better try one out prior to laying out the kind of cash that they were asking for a 45. Bill was totally for sure and was trying his best to assure Art that this was definitely the right move.   Art had always been more than a fair shot at qualifying; but was more than a little concerned with the size and recoil of this gun. However, when he stepped up and started running off a few rounds, he practically fell in love with the 45. Back in the showroom they looked several over closely and Bill finally agreed with Art on a midsized 45. They took this pistol into the range and within a few minutes Art could run a full clip into a very tight grouping. Next Art needed the quick access holster that fit snugly behind his right hip and a rather stylish belt to complete the new rig. The little 38 had been a faithful companion to Art for many a year, with just one failing, but it was a failing that none would soon forget. Now his faithful little friend would belong to the gun store and Art had his new prize at his side. Their next stop was at the police range; where the new police cadets were in the middle of their firearms training. Art watched with Bill for a little while and then asked

one of the instructors if he could possibly qualify with
his new service pistol. The man was rather impressed
with the midsized 45 and in short order Art showed
him that he could easily qualify with this new weapon.
Of course on Monday the Captain and most of the
others there had to see the new pistol. The Captain
told him that he was proud to see him with something
a little better than what he had been carrying all these
years.

     That week they purposely dug through the cold
case files that had been assigned Art and pulled out the
one where three men had pulled the armed robbery of
a bank. The report indicated that they had gotten away
clean, without hardly any leads at all. The heist had
jointly earned the three of them around seventy
thousand dollars and nothing had been found of the
stolen money. Then about two days after the heist, the
police were dispatched on a shots fired call; where two
of the would-be robbers were found shot to death.
Thomas and Little had been the detectives assigned
and they usually didn't do a very good job at all at
gathering the evidence. Art was concerned that
practically the only thing they would have to go on
was the location and the slugs pulled from the dead
men. Bill had hoped to find something that might have
his brother's scent on it or possibly something else.

     At about this same time they received a call and
were finally catching a lead on their first case. It would
seem as though one of the people they had talked with
had just received a letter from one of the ones they
were looking for. Art checked out a car from the City
Car Pool and this car was almost a joke; but it was the
best they could come up with at this short a notice.
Picking the car up, they headed off across town to a
rather old apartment complex. Just as they pulled up
in front of the apartments, the car gave up its last gasp

of life. After recovering the letter; Art had to use his new fangled cell phone, which was only assigned to him just last week, to call the station. The car was left there and he was instructed to take the City Bus back to the station. From where they were presently located, they had to walk almost five blocks to the nearest bus stop. At that point Art had to look the bus map over carefully, to see just how they could end up near the Police Station. This involved changing busses three times and practically caused them to circle the entire city. Actually they were enjoying themselves and seeing a portion of the city that Art had rarely seen. Bill loved the bus and definitely wanted to stick his head out the window. He told Art that they should take the bus more often, as it was certainly better than taking the cars from the City Car Pool. Two bus changes later; the driver was not so congenial and really didn't want the dog on her bus at all. Art insisted and the driver reluctantly caved in to police pressure. However, when it came to the dog hanging his head out the window, she felt that was just pushing things way too far. Bill then took a seat next to Art and didn't cause any further problems for the moment. That was at least until a particular man got on at one of the bus stops. The bus was about half full and Art had sat away from the people, just so Bill wouldn't bother anyone. The only seats available were next to or across from them; so the man sat down facing Art. In no time at all it seemed as if the man had recognized Art, as he managed a strained smiled.

After a few minutes Art heard, "He has a gun on his right side and is carrying a good amount of meth on his person. I'll distract him."

Art would have rather just known about this situation without actually doing anything; as there was no real proof of any of this. Bill jumped down, then up next to the man and started growling. The man turned in his seat and his hand instinctively went towards the pistol he had secreted in his right waist band. Art was quick though and in a split instant had his new 45 pointed directly at the man's chest.

With this the man was way more interested in Art than the small dog. He said, "Art, its Roy from the property room."

This was not anyone that Art had ever recognized from the property room and he just wasn't going to simply take this man's word for it. "I don't know you and haven't ever seen you before that I can remember."

"Yes Art, about a week ago I passed by while you and your dog were down there, remember."

What Art remembered about that particular day was that some of the drugs were missing and now he had a supposed property room clerk in front of him with drugs and a weapon. Art said, "Just don't make a move and back-up will be here soon enough to clear all this up." Art hoped that someone there on the bus was calling the cops as they spoke and they would quickly be on their way. After all, pandemonium had now struck and the mere sight of a gun just seemed to cause people to go crazy.

The man spoke-up, "Come on Art, give me a break."

"Then tell me why it is that you're stealing drugs from the property room," Art asked?

With this revelation the man knew that Art was on to him and he now desperately had to do something. "I had to; I was in to them for way too much. At first it was almost nothing, but the more I did the more they expected. I should have known just how this would have ended."

"Just keep your hands where I can see them. Possibly you can cut a deal and wear a wire for us," Art added.

"No, I'm a dead man anyway you look at it now," he replied; as he quickly made a grab for his pistol and Art put one round dead center. The man's gun fell from his grip and the people on the bus now went into mass hysteria. Once they were all safely off the bus, the whole situation seemed to settle right down and the police finally arrived. This definitely wasn't what Art had in mind for today, but it just happened. Well at least Bill caused it to happen. Art found a place to sit down and Bill was all excited about what had just happened. To Bill they had just done great things; but to Art, he had just taken the life of someone he didn't even know. The difference now was that Bill no longer felt any compassion for human life at all.

Art asked him, "Doesn't it bother you in the least that I just had to kill someone?"

"Not really," he heard. "Besides, that guy forced you to shoot him. It wasn't exactly as if you really had any real choices in the matter. I am impressed though with the ability of that new 45 of yours to stop people with just one shot."

The investigation into this matter was incredible; as now the property room had been compromised and everything had to be retested. The identities of the ones getting the drugs were never discovered; but all had a very good idea. It would seem that particular drugs were targeted in the property room, involving cases centered around certain individuals. What Roy couldn't know was that his usefulness had drawn to an end and he was already slated to be terminated this very day. Then the various attorneys started insisting that they be able to have the drugs privately tested, as they certainly didn't want any loose ends coming back on their clients. Certain individuals ended up with their charges being dismissed now, due to a lack of evidence.

This time however, the only one saying thank you to Art was the Captain; as Art had now shown that he was back in action once again and did not need to be drug along by anyone. Art used this opportunity to hit the Captain up for an assigned car and was turned down due to the fact that he did not have a partner. Yes and a small spotted dog didn't count as a partner. Art pointed out that he now had a lead on one of their cold cases and would need a car to travel to Gulf Port to do some follow-up. The Captain actually could care less about the cold cases; as there were more than enough current ones to go around for everyone.

He looked at Art and said, "I have a young officer that the department is pushing me to fast track through the detective's bureau and no one wants to be assigned to work with him. If you will take him on as your partner and bring him along; I'll promise you that I'll get a car assigned to you."

This wasn't exactly what Art wanted to hear, but it did allow him access to a usable vehicle. He worried about how Bill would work out with this new partner and just how well the two of them would even get along. To Art at least, taking a partner was almost like taking a wife; as one had to trust and fully count on the other constantly.

Art looked at the Captain and asked, "Just what does he know and what can he do?"

"Well he graduated out of Ole Miss with a master's degree in law, went off to advanced crime scene training, and is the Governors favorite nephew."

It was that last qualification that absolutely meant the most to Art. He was well aware that with this young man as his partner, they could have about anything they wanted.

He agreed to take the young officer on and started to leave the Captain's Office when he heard, "Finish up what you now have started in the cold cases, as I'll be putting the two of you on the rotation list."

The Captain wanted to say something about the dog, but felt that with time this issue too would work itself out. Then he hollered out as Art was walking away, "Don't you even want to know his name or when he'll be here?"

Looking back, Art commented, "Will it be before or after the new car?"

"Get out of here," the Captain yelled, with a smile.

Chapter Five

Art went home early that day and asked Sue
Ann if she would like to take a trip with him to the
coast. He really needed to use their personal car to
travel to Gulf Port and possibly they could even make
a three day weekend trip out of this same situation.
Sue Ann was ready for a trip alone with Art and told
him she could be packed in short order.

Meanwhile, Bill was out checking his domain to
make sure the cat was not out there bothering the birds
or squirrels. He had chased the cat from the yard a few
of times to this point. In fact it had become great fun
now that he was bigger and much faster. He was so
fast that could almost catch the cat, but he wasn't that
dumb. The cat on the other hand had taken to lying up
on the railing of the neighbor's deck, which would
place him just out of Bill's reach. From this lofty perch
he could taunt the dog and had on many occasions. It
wasn't this particular neighbor's cat; but the cat just
made himself at home wherever he fairly well pleased.
Bill had a belly full of this nonsense and took off for the
spot where the cat lay sleeping in the warm sunshine.
When he reached the deck, a very large leap, a bank off
of the deck leg and this put him eye level with the cat.
He then just started barking really loud and the cat
went absolutely berserk. It would have been one of the
funniest things he had ever seen, if it weren't for the cat
crap all over his face. Yes, that cat was jet propelled
and Bill had been hit directly in the face with the
exhaust. He was now running all over, rubbing his
face all over the grass and whining pathetically. The
cat however had now hopped back up on the deck
railing and was having a really good laugh at Bill's

expense. Bill had all of this he could stomach and headed straight for the doggie door. One pass through where Gina was sitting and she quickly had hold of Bill. She was holding him out at arm's length and practically threw him out the back door. When Bill tried to get back in, he found that now even the doggie door had been closed. The cat was about to bust a gut and all Bill could do was sit there on the deck in shame.

Gina quickly went in to where her dad was and said, "Something is horribly wrong, Bill stinks and I locked him outside."

Art didn't know what Bill had got himself into, but just figured that a bath was inevitable. Not having anything except for a hose outside to wash the dog with; he decided to risk it and bring him in the house for a shower. Art enlisted the help of Teddy to hold the door for him; as he went out to pick Bill up. Bill was embarrassed and didn't want to even get close to Art; so he took off and wasn't letting Art near him. It would have been almost comical seeing Art chase the dog around the back yard, if Bill just didn't stink so much.

Art was even getting quite vocal with Bill, but wasn't hearing anything in return to assure him that Bill understood a word he said. Finally with Art thoroughly worn out, he sat down on the deck.

Bill came over close and Art heard, "I really messed things up this time and the cat crapped all over me." He told Art what he had done and Art almost bust a gut himself laughing.

Then Art asked, "Well what are we going to do about this?"

"I don't know; why were you chasing me?"

"I was hoping to pick you up, take you inside and give you a shower," he replied.

Bill got up, walked over to where Art was seated and climbed up in his lap. Then Art heard, "Thank you partner."

Bill really stunk bad and Art was almost at the point of throwing up; as he took him in the house and climbed in the shower with him, clothes and all. The warm water and shampoo were flowing, and Art couldn't keep from getting some of the soap in Bill's eyes. Once they were both clean, Art stepped out of the shower and told Bill that he had to stay in the shower and shake off.

Art heard, "I just never figured that we would ever be showering together, ever."

Bill took off for the back door at a dead run and instantly came to a stand-still.

He came back in to where Art was getting dressed and Art heard, "Art old buddy, would you mind letting me out."

"What's wrong with the doggie door," he asked?

"It stinks and I don't want to smell like that again."

Art replied, "Alright, I'll clean it this time, but I don't want this to happen again."

Bill thought, "But I really didn't plan on this happening this time."

"Well then, stay well away from that cat and it won't happen again," Art added.

Art cleaned the doggie door and Bill was right, it stunk. Then he went in to where Sue Ann was and told her that he was sure sorry he took so long in getting ready. After that he explained about having to wash the dog. Sue Ann wanted to know what was wrong with Bill and Art told her she really didn't want to know.

Then Sue Ann remarked, "I know that you wanted to make this get away special for just the two of us, but Gina has a date and this is the first one since her divorce was finalized. She asked if we would mind watching Teddy before she even knew what we were planning. Would you mind greatly if we took Teddy along? I know it would mean a lot to Gina"

Art was feeling about as low as he could get at this point, using a business trip as a get away with his wife, so he came clean with what he was doing. Sue Ann didn't say much except that she and Teddy would be ready in an hour. The trip started off and not much was said between the two of them.

Finally, Sue Ann spoke-up, "Art, I'm afraid that you might get seriously hurt or possibly even killed if you stay on the force much longer."

She wondered if there might be anything that he could possibly do to get away from working for the Police Department. Art reminded her that he only had three years left and then he could retire. If he changed jobs this late in life, he would easily have to work an additional ten years.

Sue Ann added, "But at least you would be alive to retire."

"Don't worry my love," he replied.

He was trying to belay her fears; as he laid out his new master plan in detail. He told her of his new partner, about him being the Governor's nephew and then he lied. He told Sue Ann that the Captain had assured him that they would be assigned the easier cases and his job should not be anywhere near as dangerous in the future.

Bill was in the back seat with Teddy, who had fallen fast asleep, and he had heard every word. His only thoughts were, "Liar, liar, pants on fire."

Art just looked back and frowned at Bill before saying, "If that dog ever gets into that stinking stuff again, we'll just take him to the pound."

Then he actually heard Sue Ann's thoughts once more, "That would be the day."

They traveled on down to Gulf Port and decided to get Art's business out of the way first. The cold case that Art had been working on involved four young girls from Jackson, Mississippi. These four for some unknown reason had moved to Morningwood and had rented an absolute mansion. All of these girls were from well to do families and money just didn't seem to be an issue for them. The four were suppose to be in nursing school, where all had at least registered and started classes. However, none of them were attending classes at the time of the murder. The old case report was not very complete in that respect at all. Many were the kids that had went off to school on their parents money, only to find that partying took all their efforts. In fact, the only interview with the three surviving girls was one halfway completed the day they discovered the body of their friend. The particular woman that Art was interested in talking with in Gulf Port was one of those three girls who had lived there in the mansion with the dead girl, Loraine. He noticed that there was no mention of cocaine in the report, but Bill had definitely smelled cocaine on several of the pieces of evidence. He was in hopes that after all these years it would make talking about this easier and the mere mention of the cocaine perchance might spark a comment. They stopped in at the rest home in Gulf Port where Rene supposedly worked and sure enough she was not there this day. The individuals there told Art that she called in sick on a regular basis; as it seemed that she had been plagued with arthritis. Art learned the location of the apartment where she lived and it was only about five long blocks away. Showing up at Rene's apartment; Art and Bill went up to the door and Art knocked. In a fairly short amount of time a woman came to the door and asked who it was. Art introduced himself and at this point wasn't hearing anything from Bill. The woman introduced herself as Rene and asked Art if he would like to come in. Art knew how old that Rene should have been, but this woman looked to be maybe twenty years older than she should be. However, things seemed to be going good at this point and there was not even any question to why Bill was even there.

She offered him a place to sit and then asked, "How may I help you?"

Art told her about his reopening the cold case into Loraine's death and the fact that he had learned that she was one of the other three girls living there in the mansion with Loraine at that time.

The woman just looked down, which he knew was not a good sign, and asked, "What can I help you with?"

Art still had not heard anything from Bill, as he asked, "If you wouldn't mind, I would like to hear about your life there with Loraine?"

Rene started in and told a very interesting story with basically no problems at all. Art knew that anyone telling a story without problems was basically lying; as life just wasn't that way. He broke it to her about the cocaine and she drew back as if to say no more.

Then after a few quiet and fairly reflective moments, she drew in closer to say, "I really didn't want to sully the memory of my friend Loraine. But seeing that you already know about her cocaine usage; I might as well tell you that we were terribly surprised to learn what she was doing. Just imagine cocaine of

all things. Drugs just weren't one of the things that us
girls would have ever been caught doing."

Art asked, "You wouldn't have any idea where
she was getting her cocaine would you?"

"Yes," she replied, "from a sleazy low life by the
name of Jason Roberts."

Then Art broke the big question, "Who do you
think killed her?"

"Well in my opinion it was ether Jason or that
no good for nothing partner of his, John Learsey."

"Why do you say that," Art asked?

"Because drugs lead to nothing good and they
were trading sex for drugs with Loraine."

Art asked, "You wouldn't happen to know
where a person might find Jason Roberts or John
Learsey would you?"

Loraine paused and then slowly answered, "I
believe that Jason is living fairly near here; somewhere
around Slidell I hear."

Art didn't ask how she knew this and regretted
not asking this question in fairly short order. He did
ask in parting though, just what four nursing students
were doing renting a rather large mansion. Rene told
him that they were bleached blonde, stupid, and well
financed by their parents. At one point Bill commented
to Art that the entire place reeked of the smell of
methamphetamines and likely Rene was using her
arthritis as a cover-up for her drug habit.

When they returned to the car, Art told Sue Ann
that they needed to go visit with just one more
individual. He explained that he had been told that the
man lived just a few miles from there and she seemed
to be at least alright with this situation. Back there at
Rene's apartment; Sue Ann told Art that they would
wait in the car and she also thought she included Bill in
this comment. However, Art even opened the back

door and said, "Come on Bill," when they arrived. Her
husband had really changed since he and Bill had
bonded, and she worried constantly that something
would happen to change this situation.

Traveling to Slidell, Art thought it best to check-
in with the local authorities first; especially since they
were now in Louisiana. Just possibly they could point
him in the direction of Jason Roberts. As it turned out
this was a good choice, because Jason just happened to
be in for a lengthy stay at the local Parish Jail. The
officers there were very accommodating to Art and
didn't even give him much static over taking Bill in
with him. They were taken to a private visitation room
and were let in to visit face to face with Jason. Almost
instantly Bill started smelling weed and in short order
had narrowed it down to Jason's socks.

With this information, Art introduced himself
and asked Jason if he would like to visit with him.
Jason was far from being the typical inmate and
wanted to know from the onset just what was in it for
him.

Smiling really big, Art leaned forward and said,
"Well maybe you could keep yourself out of further
trouble by pointing us in the proper direction. Or
possibly I could just get that nice guard back in here to
remove the marijuana from your socks."

Jason sat there for a moment and then said,
"Man that's just not right; bringing a drug dog in here
the way you did to set me up. If I get busted once
more it'll add a year to my sentence."

"A year is incredibly minor compared to what I
need to talk with you about," Art added.

It would seem as though Loraine had been hit in
the head with a hammer, stabbed once in the upper
back with an ice pick and had a cord tied tightly
around her neck.

These items had various smells to them and Art hoped that Bill might key in on the killer, if he could just have a chance at smelling the subjects involved. There were four girls in the house and of course their odors would definitely be all over everything. The problem was not in having just one odor to put an owner with, but rather several odors. Bill had already made the determination that Jason's odor was not on any of the weapons used and this should definitely cause Jason to want to help them. With a promise from Art that he would not mention the weed in his socks, Jason at least agreed to visit with him. They discussed the time when the murder happened and just who all were involved with the girls at that particular time. Jason was really able to enlighten Art; as it seems as though the girls had rented that particular mansion for a very specific reason. It had four separate living quarters off of a central common area and these young girls were running a very successful courtesan service out of that mansion. He told Art that even though the girls were only about twenty; each had their own BMW, diamonds everywhere, and they dressed like they were very high society. He allowed that theirs was definitely a first class operation.

Art was writing everything down and finally caught up with all the information that Jason had given him. He didn't have to worry about taking his eyes off of Jason; as his other pair of eyes were trained on everything Jason did and was constantly reporting back to Art. It was very surprising to Art that the original officers had not picked up on this situation; as they said nothing of this in their original reports.

He asked Jason where John Learsey had gone off to and Jason had no idea other than to say, "Probably in a shallow grave somewhere."

"Oh, and would you possibly know where," Art asked?

Jason replied, "Not really, as the last time I saw that bastard he had a gun pointed at me and was robbing me."

"Do you think he could have been involved in the death of Loraine," Art asked?

"No, it definitely was one of those other three girls," he commented. "They really didn't like the fact that Loraine was involved with John or me."

Art asked, "You wouldn't happen to know where I might find these women, would you?"

"Well now, for about twenty dollars, I might just get some information flowing through this old brain of mine; on just where two of them might be located," he slyly remarked.

Looking right at him, Art said, "Then our original deal is off and we need to renegotiate. I was actually planning on sticking by my promise; but if that's not what you want, then maybe we need to start afresh."

Jason spoke-up, "Our original deal is just fine by me, but you at least can't fault me for trying. Rene can be found in Gulf Port and Betty is just over in Gretna."

Art remembered to ask this time just how he knew this and Jason told him that they had been steady customers of his over the last several years. This was finally starting to make some sense now; as three weapons were used and there were the three of them. In fact, Rene had only pointed him towards Jason with the hope that it would take some of the suspicion off of them. Surely she just didn't plan of Jason being so cooperative. Art now had to go with hat in hand and ask Sue Ann if it would be alright for them to go on over to New Orleans, as Gretna was basically a suburb across the river.

Once more Sue Ann was more than receptive to this idea; but insisted that Art leave her and Teddy off in the French Quarters, prior to his going on over to Gretna. Art once more checked in with the local authorities and again it was very beneficial. He learned that Betty was actually living as a homeless woman in an area of Gretna and they fairly well knew where she could be located. The officers told him not to expect much from her; as she mumbled a lot and would often ramble on about her being a beauty queen. No one could possibly believe that now, from the way she currently looked. Art had no trouble finding her and couldn't believe that a woman that young could actually look that bad without the use of theatrical makeup. In his previous investigations, he had learned just what the homeless would do absolutely anything for; so he stopped off and bought a carton of cigarettes, two bottles of cheap wine, and a double handful of chocolate bars. Walking up to Betty, he immediately wished that he had also bought some dip; as she spat almost on his shoes.

He told her who he was and even told her what it was that he was investigating. In the mean time, Bill kept repeating over and over that her odor was on the cord which had been pulled tightly around Loraine's neck. At first Betty would try to walk away and wanted nothing to do with him; that was until he started pulling out the chocolate bars. She at least took the time now to take some of the candy from his hand. He reached in his bag once more, brought out a pack of cigarettes and she immediately wanted these also. Handing her the pack of cigarettes, she now was very interested in just what else he had in that bag.

Art closed the bag and said, "We talk first and then it's all yours." She started to walk away and he said, "Well would you look at this," as he pulled a bottle of the cheap wine partially up out of the bag.

Art now had Betty's undivided attention and she said, "But not here, let's go somewhere that all can't see what I have." She glared at Bill and said, "Does the dog have to come along?"

"It's both of us or nothing," Art replied.

They walked down the street to an opening between two rather old houses; which was rather overgrown with vines and Betty proceeded straight through the narrow opening in the vines. Immediately Bill followed her through and Art heard that everything looked to be alright. Art stooped over and when he came through the vines there was Betty standing there waiting on the other side.

She asked, "Just what is it that you hope to get from me?"

"Possibly a confession," Art replied.

"A confession to what," she demanded?

He looked her right in the eyes and said, "We know that the three of you killed Loraine and it was you that put the cord around her neck."

She sighed, took a deep breath and almost looked relieved. Then she sat down on a stone ledge and said, "Well it's been a long time in coming, but I'm glad that it's finally here."

Art asked her, "Do you want to tell me the whole story about the four of you being prostitutes or such?"

"No, never prostitutes or at least we didn't look at it as such in those days," she replied. "Let's see, just where should I start." Pausing for a moment, Betty looked up at Art and started in, "The whole situation actually started out at the end of our junior year back in high school. The four of us girls were from extremely wealthy families, who really weren't

interested in us in the least. We had one definite fact
in common and that was that we were all middle
children. Our parents were just too tied up with
everything else in their lives; so they just poured
money on us to keep us out of their hair. At least at
first it was all Karen's idea; as she was the great thinker
of the group. We had already shared a lot throughout
the years and she always came up with such wonderful
ideas. However, we felt that her latest idea was
probably one of her best. Us four girls rented a house
in Jackson and practically moved in there without any
of our parent's knowledge. Of course if anyone in the
families ever asked, we were always staying the night
with one of the other girls. What we accomplished at
that house was no less than a teen strip club. We
would dance and even paid several of the other girls
from school to dance there. Of course our strip club
didn't have to abide by any of the rules and the
dancers always ended up dancing totally nude. It's a
good thing that people didn't carry cameras back in
those days, or all hell would have broken loose.
Admittance was by personal invite only and there was
a $50.00 cover charge. When the girls got down to just
their underwear, the patrons would shove lots of
money in these skimpy garments, if they wanted them
to come off. Several of the girls made extra money
giving lap dances and such. But then we figured out
where the real money was and fairly quickly moved
away from the dancing. By the end of our senior year
Karen had a totally new plan for us and all of us were
in agreement. That was when we visited
Morningwood and found absolutely the perfect place.
We sold our overly rich parents on the idea of us going
off to nursing school and most were just glad that we
were going to do anything with our lives. Once again
it was Karen's grand idea and we all entered into a

new pledge with one another. This time we agreed
that everything that we made off of our courtesan
business would go into a common pot and all would
share equally in the rewards. When I say that we had
discovered where the real money was, I mean that we
had moved into a very high class business and
entertained no one for less than three hundred dollars
per guest. After being in business for only a year; we
all drove BMW sportsters, wore the finest of clothes,
and pampered ourselves in any manner that we could.
We were now able to raise our rates; as our clients now
included individuals as high up in the Morningwood
society as those in the Mayor's very office. Karen had
made all of us firmly pledge that we would drink
moderately, never use drugs of any sort, and would
share everything equally. This agreement slowly fell
by the wayside for most of us, but I do not believe that
Karen ever used any drugs. Life at that point couldn't
have been better; when Rene and I received a visit this
one day from Karen. She was carrying with her a
hammer, an ice pick and a cord. She told us that
Loraine had been holding out on us and she needed to
be taught a lesson. We followed Karen to Loraine's
room where there was about twenty thousand dollars
laying out on her bed, along with about a quarter of a
pound of what looked to be cocaine. Karen informed
us that it was time to bring in a new and more
trustworthy partner into our partnership. We sat there
on the edge of Loraine's bed counting the money and I
didn't actually know just what Karen was talking
about. Loraine came in at about that time and started
screaming for us to get out of her room and how we
had no business going through her personal
belongings. That was when Karen picked up the
hammer and hit her in the back of the head. Loraine
fell face forward into the money as Karen just pointed

at the cord and ice pick. Rene quickly grabbed up the ice pick and slammed it into Loraine's back. It was too late for me to back out now; so I took the cord and put it around Loraine's neck. I hadn't pulled it tight enough to suit Karen, so she pushed me aside and pulled it up very tight. At about that time Karen told us to make it look like it was a robbery gone horribly wrong. We split up the cash, went through everything she had and took anything of value. Of course no one could prove that any of these items weren't ours, as we all had the same things. I absolutely thought that Karen was actually going to pull Loraine's finger off; getting that five carat diamond ring off her finger. By this time Loraine's body was jerking about and I just wanted to be out of there. We left everything in disarray and decided to all go out for the evening. In this manner we could all be each other's alibi. That following morning our house keeper found Loraine and started screaming. We came into her room and all went over to the body like we were really concerned for our friend's safety. Then we called the cops and you should pretty well know how that went. However, our problems really got started that evening when Jason and John came around looking for Loraine. They pretty well summed up what we had done and wanted their money back. We couldn't actually admit to having killed Loraine and besides Karen had flushed the remainder of their drugs down the toilet. John told us that he knew what we had done and as a result we were now going to have to work off Loraine's debt, or end up just like her. By the time they left that evening they had it all figured out; they would just take over our little business and we would prostitute for them. Karen wasn't about to go there and neither Rene nor I wanted this either. By early the next morning we had our prized possessions loaded in our Beamers and all

took off in separate directions. Finally I heard that
Rene had ended up in Florida, before making her way
back to Gulf Port. Me, I came to New Orleans and was
dancing in the clubs in no time at all. I took on a show
name and Betty was a thing of the past. Slowly but
surely I even started prostituting and then it happened,
I got AIDS. Now my days are numbered and I'm glad
to have this off my soul before I leave."

Art handed her the bag, which she immediately
examined carefully. Then she asked, "Will I now be
going to jail for this?"

"Not today," Art commented. "But I will need a
complete statement on this matter if you wouldn't
mind."

"That'll be fine," she added, "as prison is much
more preferable than where I am now. I understand
that the food over there in the Mississippi prison is
fairly good. I will gain a roof over my head, a soft bed,
and three meals a day. Sounds like a good place to end
my days."

Art and Bill left her to her new treasure and
started walking back towards the car. Everything was
fairly quiet, as neither of them could believe just how
badly people could screw up their lives. Betty's idea of
treasure had gone from BMWs and diamonds to
cigarettes, chocolates, and cheap wine.

Chapter Six

With this completed, Art's little group could actually look forward to a leisurely weekend or at least what was left of it. They proceeded back to the Mississippi coast and easily found a place to stay. It was getting late evening and everyone was hungry. The man at the motel told them where they could find some wonderful oyster PoBoys and Sue Ann was ready. It had been many years since she had found anyone that could actually make a good one and these were wonderful. They purchased an order of roast beef for Bill and everyone was set for the evening. Later on that night they walked along the beach at low tide, while Teddy and Bill played in the shallow water. Teddy experienced many wonderful things that night; jelly fish that glowed when a light hit them and crabs so soft that he could easily pick one up without being pinched.

The family had enjoyed a full day together and everyone was ready for bed; but Art just couldn't sleep. Art's mind was trying to assimilate this case and he decided that he needed to once more go visit with Rene.

That next morning Bill and Art were up before the others and decided to slip off to talk with Rene. This time they found her at work and for some reason she just didn't seem surprised. They sat down in a quiet area and Rene had her head down.

All sat there quietly for a moment and then she asked, "When did you find out?"

Art of course lied and said, "We had a fair idea before we came down here. You know, three suspects and three murder weapons."

She replied, "I didn't want to do it, but I didn't see any way out with Karen standing there with that hammer still in her hand. I just grabbed up that ice pick and couldn't believe how easily it sunk into Loraine's back. I didn't stab her but once though."

Art didn't tell her that the crime lab determined that the blow to the head had cracked her skull, the stab wound missed everything but a lung, and it was the cord that had actually ended her life. Rene agreed to go with them to the local police station and give them a full statement. On the way there however, she must have had other thoughts; as she jumped from the moving vehicle and broke her neck. That pretty well destroyed the remainder of that day and Art was almost afraid to return to the motel. Sue Ann had at least received a call from him and was fairly put out at first. But by the time that Art arrived, she had recalled how things had been for the past year and was pleased that he was out there doing his job. At least one good thing had come from this situation; as Art and his entire family had been invited to a local law enforcement gathering.

They all enjoyed a wonderful evening; as there was plenty beer, raw oysters, boiled crawfish and a combination of other foods too numerous to even mention. Art talked Bill into trying a raw oyster and Bill decided that it tasted like cat food. When Art peeled a crawfish tail for him though, there was no mention of what it tasted like, but rather it went straight on down. Sue Ann couldn't believe that Art was just sitting there peeling crawfish for the dog; after all the fits he had thrown in the past about feeding the dog from the table. They made some lasting friendships that evening and everything reminded them of when they had the weekend parties at their old home.

Heading back home the next day; Sue Ann told
Art that, in spite of everything, she had a wonderful
time with him this weekend. That next week at work
all found out that Art had now solved his first cold case
and the Captain was very pleased. The family of the
dead girl had not let anyone forget, even after all these
years, that their daughter's killer was still out there
somewhere. With the closure of this case, they should
have found some peace in knowing just who it was
that had murdered their daughter.

However, with the revelation of what all had
happened in this situation, no one gained any peace.
Instead, the parents became very hateful and
demanded that their daughter's killers be brought to
justice. Art learned that Loraine's BMW had been left
at the mansion there in Morningwood at the time of
her death. Her family had tried to take it and ended up
in a horrible battle with the lender; who was still owed
most of the value of the car. The BMW dealer told Art
that they had found two of the other cars abandoned,
one in Florida and one in New Orleans. However, one
of the girls came in and just left her car there at the
dealership. Then about a week later a man came in
and wanted to know what they wanted for the used
BMW. He paid cash and they were so glad to get it
that they didn't even push him for his name. That was
alright though; as Art could run a nationwide search
on the Vehicle Identification Number. The results
came back as not found in the system, so he decided to
search back in the records to the year following
Loraine's death. Here he actually got results; as the car
had been titled that year in North Carolina to a
Caroline Woodridge. The address came back to a Mr.
and Mrs. Thomas Woodridge. One call later and he
found out that Caroline Woodridge was actually the
Karen he was looking for. Mr. Woodridge was rather

informative and told him that they never were actually married. It had seemed to him back then that Karen was running away from something and he had allowed her to assume the name Caroline Woodridge. He told Art that she had really taken to drinking over the next two years and had totally became a lush. In fact they had fairly well went their separate ways, when he heard that she had wrapped her car around a tree somewhere up near Boston. It was his understanding that she had really messed herself up good this time.

Art was finally ready to start his second cold case, when Bill jumped up on the desk and he heard, "Art, would you please look at the armed robbery case where two of the robbers were found dead the following day."

"In other words, the one involving your brother, right," Art asked?

For a few seconds Art wasn't picking up on anything and then he heard. "Yes, you see if we could prove that it was him, this would make things a lot easier and safer for my sister."

"Well, I always knew that there had to be a reason for you're coming back the way you did and this is that reason." Art replied. "But if we do this, then will that change things between us?"

He heard, "No, my sister wasn't the reason for me coming back this way, it was you Art and always will be."

Art grabbed his little dog up and hugged him tightly, "Don't leave me, because without you I'm nothing." Wiping away some tears, Art said, "Then let's get that bastard for you and your sister."

Bill was looking around at this time and just hoped that no one was watching.

They proceeded down to the property room and checked out everything collected in that particular case.

There was a tremendous amount of material and several items where that DNA could be compared, if only there was a suspect. Looking through everything, there truly was no direction to go from here; as every aspect of this case had been thoroughly looked into. The only possible lead was a girl that had been seen coming from the room of the two dead robbers. She had not been identified at that time and possibly someone else at the apartment building might have also seen her or remembered something about her. When Bill and Art arrived at the apartment complex, they found the building to be a rather large and totally rundown structure. Down the sides of the building lay actual parts of this building that had fallen off over the years. Entering through the half broken front door, they found that the place was even more rundown on the inside than it looked to be on the outside, if that was at all possible. There was a short filthy looking bald man behind the counter swatting flies; while a rather large yellow cat lay listlessly up on the counter.

Before anything was even said, the man behind the counter informed them, "There are no pets allowed here." Art pointed at the cat on the counter and in turn he man pointed at a fly. He then swatted the fly and said, "Swatter for the flies and cat for the rats."

Art pulled out his credentials and the man got even quieter. Everything in the world had happened there at one time or another and now just what exactly did this cop want?

Pointing at the register, Art asked, "Would you mind if we took a look at that?"

Pushing it across the counter the man said, "Knock yourself out, but don't take it from the counter without a warrant."

"A bit testy aren't you, for a person that shouldn't have anything to hide," Art remarked?

"You would be too if a cop had stolen something from you," he remarked.

"What would a cop steal from this place," Art asked?

The man looked him in the face, pulled the book back and then said, "My last book, are you dense?"

"Just when did that happen," Art asked?

"That was just before they found those two dead men in apartment 31," he added.

Now Art was really interested and asked, "How did you know that he was a cop?"

"Flashed one of those fancy tin badges just like you did," he replied.

"Did you tell the officers that came here to work the homicide," Art inquired?

"Sure did, and they thought that I was lying. They accused me of housing illegals and druggies without keeping a record. Oh I told them just what I thought of them and said that they could get the record off of that other cop, if they ever found him."

Art knew most of the officers that had ever worked in Morningwood, so he asked, "Can you tell me anything about that other cop?"

"Well let's see, I had seen him around here a few times before he asked for the book, but he didn't really look like a cop. Then the day that he flashed his badge, he had a woman with him. He would be hard to describe, but if I saw that woman again, I believe that I would recognize her for sure."

Art reached down and real slow like picked Bill up, just so that he could see the register.

The man asked, "He doesn't chase cats does he?"

Once more Art lied and said, "No, never, he and cats are best friends."

Bill heard this and cringed, but knew that he had to do this for his sister's sake.

This new book started at about the time of the homicides and would only be of benefit in letting them know who had been there at that time and what rooms were leased after that point. Art couldn't believe that the only accounting records that this fool had, was a simple mark by the room number to show who had paid their rent that month, in cash. Looking through the records he noticed that most of the people had signed the book in such a manner that no one could read their names, even if they needed too. Art and Bill were getting a feeling for what the homicide detectives had run into on their original investigation. With what had been done at that time, Bill got a greater appreciation for what detectives Thomas and Little had actually done. The old building had forty-eight small apartments for lease and always seemed to stay rather full. Some of the individuals living there had been there forever, and then there were others who came and went within a month or more. It was evidently going to be a long exhaustive search, but these two were dedicated to this endeavor. Many of the ones living in these squalid of circumstances simply left their kids unsupervised during the day and were only around at night. Others had learned to just flat not come to the door, no matter who was out there knocking. One thing about this situation though, Art was able to tell if someone was moving around in the apartment with the aid of Bill's superior hearing ability. Not only that, but he was also hearing Bill's read on just what was in each apartment. Bill would make a simple sniff at the crack under the door and Art would start hearing his report. Sometimes it was as simple as what they were having for lunch, and then at other times it was drugs or even worse.

At one particular apartment Bill put his nose to the bottom of the door and then looked straight up at Art. Art heard, "Bad, someone has been dead in this apartment for a very long time."

They went back to the manager's desk and he didn't even want to open the door to the apartment for them. Art mentioned that they probably needed to get immigrations and the health department involved in this; which quickly changed the manager's mind. Upon opening the door, they found an elderly gentlemen sitting in a chair and he had been dead for at least a month now. They asked the manager why no one had noticed this and he told them that most of the people living there minded their own business. The authorities soon arrived, the scene was worked, but not by Art. Heading home that evening, Art felt that things were finally starting to unravel in this latest case; as they just needed to decide which string to pull next.

It was about two in the morning when Art felt a cool nose on his arm and heard, "I think I have it figured out now?"

Art got up and went out back with Bill, "Just what is it that you have figured out, which couldn't wait until morning?"

He heard, "When you had me circle through the old man's apartment, I noticed a few pictures and really didn't think much about it at the time. But one of the women in those pictures, for some strange reason, sure looked familiar to me. I kept trying to reflect on just where I had seen her before and then it finally came to me. When my father died, my brother brought a woman to the funeral and I got to see her face only for a few minutes at the grave site. When we all got together later, she was not there and I don't exactly remember anyone asking him where she was.

That particular night my father and sister's home was broken into and several thousand dollars worth of valuables were taken. At this same time I was staying at the home myself and lost my badge and service revolver in the burglary. This was all turned in to the Picayune Police Department at that time and none of us suspected my brother; as he was with us the entire evening."

"Well now that makes sense," Art replied. "He brings her to the funeral and gets all of you away from the home; she then breaks in and has all evening to clean the place out."

He heard, "That was one thing that bothered not only me but the Picayune Police; as they had not seen a burglar spend so much time cleaning a place out like that before. Most of the time they break-in, set a maximum of three to five minutes inside and then they're out of there."

Art asked, "Did anything from the burglary every surface?"

"Nothing," he heard, "but no one was looking for anything other than just there locally."

That following morning they returned to the old man's apartment and picked-up one of the pictures of the woman. Going down to the manager, Art asked, "Was this the woman that was with the policeman who took your ledger?"

He looked closely at the picture and said, "She very well could have been, but I don't think her hair looked like that."

Continuing their investigation by going around to all the other apartments; they received two other maybes on this woman being there at the location of the double homicide. They now felt that they had a picture of the woman, but no name to go along with it. Art sent the picture off to the department of motor vehicles; but no driver license match came back to the woman in the picture. Bill relayed to him that the woman in the picture was a brunette, but the woman at his father's funeral had sandy blonde hair. Art decided to find out where Bill's brother was now licensed to drive and they would check there to see if there could possibly be a driver's license match for this woman. Sure enough, Joseph W. Aaron was licensed in the State of Louisiana and so was Louise Renee Aaron. However, these two had separate addresses.

Art put in a call to Louise and told her of the old man's death. At first she was only interested in how he had found her; so he told her of the picture. Then she allowed that she did know the old man; as he was her father. However, she insisted that she had not seen him in over twenty years and had never been to the particular apartment where he had died. Art asked her if her husband was there and she told him that she didn't have a husband.

He said, "I heard that you might be married to my old partner's brother Joseph Aaron."

She was quiet for a few moments at that revelation; not knowing where he might have got that information. She said, "We were married, but I haven't seen him in several years now."

Art asked, "Could I possibly get you to come in visit with me about Joseph?"

"What about," she quickly asked?

"Well I would really rather talk with you in person about this matter and not over the phone," he added. "In fact it might even be financially beneficial to you."

She hesitated for a few moments and then said, "I guess I do need to come settle my father's affairs and will get with you at that time."

"Just give me a call and we can get together," he replied.

Nothing about this call gave him any further cause for concern, past the fact that he was starting to investigate a cold blooded killer. Art actually didn't expect for her to call at all and as such he and Bill would have one more trip to make down there to visit with her. He felt that the one they had better keep a sharp eye out for was JW's brother, as he was probably fairly unstable.

Chapter Seven

Bill now wanted to see his sister and used the pretext that they could look at the funeral pictures, to see if the woman just happened to get into any of the shots that were taken. JW's father's funeral had been celebrated in traditional grand style; with the wake turning into a very huge party. Several individuals had taken pictures and at least one had taken a video. Art called Lea Belle and explained to her just who he was. She was anxious to talk with her brother's expartner and invited him and his wife down for the weekend.

Sue Ann was also excited about meeting JW's sister and was glad once more to be getting away with Art. Upon suggesting that they leave Bill at home, she got the look. She knew that look and pursued this matter no further. Their time spent down at Picayune was wonderful and Lea Belle insisted that they stay at her home. There was no mention of Bill even being with them; but she thought it odd to invite someone as a guest, just to have them show-up with their dog. As the weekend wore on though, Lea Belle became very impressed with this dog; as he was no trouble at all and seemed to take in everything that was being said. Being somewhat of a liberal thinker, she at one point asked Art if he believed that people could actually come back as animals. Bill just kept reminding Art not to go there; as he didn't want to mess-up his sisters thinking any more than it already was. When the pictures and video finally came out; Art and Bill watched closely for the woman, who was captured only once and that was on the video.

Bill at least thought, "Yes, that's her."

After rewinding and running the film forward several times, Lea Belle asked, "Just what is it that has you so fascinated with this woman?"

Art told her that they were working on a homicide back at Morningwood and this woman may have possibly been involved.

She commented, "Joseph's wife?"

Art pulled out the picture from the old man's apartment and showed it to Lea Belle.

She exclaimed, "Yes that's her, but her hair is darker in this picture."

He hesitated for a moment, Bill was telling him over and over not to go there, and he said, "I have reason to believe that she was the one who burglarized your home back at your father's funeral."

Lea Belle replied without surprise, "I wondered if that wasn't what had happened. Surely JW must have had this same feeling and shared his suspicions with you?"

Once more Bill was almost threatening Art if he told anything, "Well its part of an active ongoing case that I'm working on and I can't really talk about it at this time."

"Sometime, when the time is right, I would like to know everything," she remarked.

That following week Art showed up for work and was introduced to Donald Ray Claybourn, his new partner. He had now completed the State's Basic Law Enforcement Academy; which just left him as the new officer on the street with a gun and a badge. However, very few officers started off their first day on the force with an actual detective's badge. The Captain gave Art one last piece of advice and that was to take very good care of this new green rookie. They spent the remainder of that week bringing him up to speed on the case that they were currently working on. Art decided that he would allow Don, as they now called him, to do the case reports on this case; being that he also had a law degree. Besides, this greatly freed up Art to do as he pleased and after all Don needed to have his name on such an important case as this. Art even invited Don home with him and told him to plan on spending the entire weekend. Don had only been staying in a motel up to this time and was dying to grow even closer to this seasoned veteran officer. Sue Ann told Art that they would get everything ready for a full weekend of partying, to give a proper welcome to the Governors' favorite nephew. When the two men finally showed up at the house; neither Art nor Sue Ann had even thought of the fact that they were bringing together a single male and single female this weekend. Don was almost immediately smitten with Gina and played constantly with Teddy. Art and Sue Ann may have been a little slow on the uptake; but soon figured out that Don would probably spend a good amount of time at their home in the future.

Then on Sunday evening, at just about dusk, Art received a call from the Departments Dispatch. The Dispatcher told him that a woman had called several times trying to get hold of him. Each time she refused to leave her name. However, this last time she said that she would be here only a few more hours if he wanted to visit with her. Art wasn't prepared to go off to work; as he and Don had both knocked back way more than a few beers and an absolutely wonderful steak. He promised both of the women that they would be back as soon as they possible could. Art fairly well knew who had called and where she would be, even without her actually having said anything. Then he called for a squad car to be sent by and the two of them were both transported across town to the apartment complex. Joseph and Louise had calculated that if they called Art on a Sunday evening, he might possibly come by himself. They parked their car out back and used the back stairs to access the floor on which her father's room had been located. Louise still had her key from before and they left the door slightly ajar. Louise hid in the bathroom and Joseph hid in the bedroom closet.

When the officers arrived at the apartments; the one that had given them the ride asked if he could come in with them. With Bill in the lead, the three officers entered the building. They asked the manager if he had let anyone in the old man's apartment and he said no. Arriving at the door they found it ajar and Bill quickly smelled the presence of his brother and a woman. He relayed this to Art and immediately went straight into the apartment. Art wasn't for sure if they had come and gone, or if they were still in there. He quickly alerted the other officers to pull their guns, as he followed Bill through the door. By this time Bill was looking for his brother and had located his odor coming from the direction of the closet. After letting Art know this, he took his foot and pulled slightly on the only partially closed closet door. Joseph had not been looking for a small dog at the bottom of the door; but rather felt that Art must have had hold of the door knob and was pulling it open. With a quick look inside; Bill saw that his brother had a rather large gun pointed directly at the door. About this time Bill lunged inside the closet and took hold of Joseph's leg. In total surprise, Joseph went ahead and pulled both barrels of the sawed off shotgun he had firmly trained on the door. The gun bellowed and blew a tremendous hole in the door very near the door knob. Wood splinters were flying everywhere. Art already had his 45 out and filled the door with holes. Joseph's body fell forward and pushed the door further open. He was still gripping the shotgun, as Art ended this matter with one fatal shot. At about this time Louise burst forth from the bathroom and put two rounds dead center in the officer closest to her. This just happened to be the patrol officer; who fortunately happened to be the only one wearing a vest. Don then emptied his 38 snub nosed revolver dead center on Louise. Needless to say this had not been the quiet evening they had planned and both men spent most of the night writing reports.

At one point Bill sat looking at his dead brother and thought that he never looked better. Now his sister would be the sole owner of her business, like it should have been from the very first.

Art was rather pleased with just how Bill had been able to unravel this trap before it was sprung. He also was pleased to hear that Bill was not upset with him for killing his brother, and very pleased with the fact that Don was a whiz with reports. Don's legal education was definitely worth every cent that his parents had paid for it.

When the Captain finally received the reports the next morning, he just looked at Art and said, "What in the world is this?"

He had never been handed such a complete report before and there was absolutely nothing that needed correcting. Don had made Art out to be the smartest detective to have ever lived and it was truly what he believed from this short time as his partner. Art knew that all the praise definitely lay with Bill's ability and made sure the Captain was aware that Bill had alerted him to the danger which awaited them just inside the apartment. When Joseph's autopsy returned, Art also had to explain just why that Joseph had bite marks on his left leg. Not only bite marks, but dogs bite marks. Once more Art was recognized for his service to the City, but this time Don and Bill were also recognized. The Captain was very pleased to be recognizing Don at this early date; as this also made him look good in the eyes of his superiors. This still did not impress Sue Ann and Gina, who definitely felt that they had a rather large stake in the outcome of this situation. Art promised them that now that he had a new partner, things would finally settle down and the Captain would definitely give them the easier cases. He came up with this due to Don's connections and just what they meant to the Captain's future plans.

Don had not been given the time to even look for a place to stay and had returned to Art's house daily without a word said about him not being welcome there. It was Gina that brought up the fact that her father's last partner, JW, had practically lived at their home. She openly suggested that they could easily rent Don a room there at the house and it would work out for the best for all concerned. Bill was letting Art know that he knew who it was that she was actually concerned about. Not only this, but Bill also was in full agreement that she and Don would make the perfect match. With no descending comments, it was decided that they now had a boarder.

That following Monday the Captain called everyone in for a meeting and announced that he was moving Art and Don into the regular Detective rotation schedule. The two Detectives with the worst case closure record were moved to cold cases; with the directive that if they could solve even one of the cold cases, they could then return to the regular rotation. The Detectives on rotation were scheduled to work eight hour shifts; leaving the morning shift as the most desirable. The Captain had not only moved Art and Don into the rotation schedule, but he had also placed them on the morning shift. This surprised Art, but he made little complaint; as most of the others were complaining enough for everyone. The other Detectives claimed that this move was directly due to Don being the Governors' nephew; but the Captain insisted that it was totally due to case closures and reports completed properly. Art and JW may have had the highest rate of case closures of any of the Detectives there on the force; but their reports left much to be desired. With the addition of Don, Art could see that things were already going to be a whole lot simpler and better. Many of the Detectives that had flatly refused to take on this new green rookie officer were now rethinking their hasty decisions. Art may have been receiving the cold shoulder treatment by his peers; but Don on the other hand was being treated as if he may have been a long lost friend or something of the such. All in all, none of them had time for interaction anyway; as the Captain had now shown that everyone's position was up for grabs.

The very first case that Art and Don were assigned was an absolute slam-dunk; which only served to better their standings and everyone knew that it would. This case came in on their rotation and no one showed any partiality in assigning this case to them. When they arrived at the motel, the manager was waiting with his key in hand and the door was still locked. The only reason that anything was even thought about this situation at all, was that the man inside had not responded to the wakeup call that he himself had requested. The clerk had already checked his records and had found the man's car to be parked directly in front of the room in question. Easing the door open, they announced themselves and it was fairly evident that the man in the bed was dead. He was sixty-eight years old and as it turned out way too rich to be staying in a motel such as this. On the nightstand next to the bed they found a bottle of whiskey and an open bottle of pills. This looked like a classic suicide, but there was no note or anything else to indicate that the man had decided to take his own life. Don immediately fell into his evidence collecting mode and Art started analyzing everything. In short order Bill declared that there had been a woman in there with him.

Art told Don, "Something is just not right about this. I believe that he had a woman in here with him."

Don stayed after it and finally declared that he had found a very long blonde hair on the man's body. Bill did his usual sniffing around and let Art know that there was something on the floor at the foot of the bed, which smelled very interesting. Art marked it for collection, as Don was systematically covering the room. While Don was finishing up, Art and Bill went around and talked with the various individuals in the other rooms. None of them had particularly seen anything of benefit and Bill hit on no smells that would tie these individuals to that room. However, one of the individuals, staying a few rooms down, complained that he had to park clean over on the other side of the motel.

He complained that this side of the motel was totally full. Art had asked if anyone had seen any prostitutes hanging around the place and it was the general consensus that they were out there every night.

The Captain felt that it looked to be a straight forward suicide and asked just why they shouldn't close this case as such. This could easily be one more case that he could chalk up to Don's credit.

Art spoke-up, "Since when does a person intent on committing suicide call down to the office and leave a wakeup call?

The Captain replied without further discussion, "Then follow-up on this, but keep me informed of everything."

Checking into the dead man's background; they found that he was from Vicksburg, was retired, and was filthy rich. He was not there on business and his young wife said that he had just left out without telling anyone where he was going. According to her he had been greatly depressed ever since retiring. She was an extremely beautiful woman, but only about thirty years old. Art was immediately concerned over the fact that this young woman stood to inherit all of this man's millions; leaving practically nothing to his children. The one thing that actually broke this whole case open was when Bill informed Art that she had been the woman in that room. Art asked her when she had last seen her husband; as it appeared as if he may have committed suicide. The woman told him that she had last seen her husband two days before; when he simply walked out without telling anyone where he was going. Art talked her into making an official statement to the facts that she had given them and knew that he now had what he needed to eventually pull her alibi completely apart. However, this woman's hair was not blonde, but rather red; so just who was it that the long blonde hair belonged to anyway?

Art asked Bill if he was certain that there had only been one woman in that room with the man. Bill let him know that several people had been in that room, but only the man and his wife within the last several hours. Possibly the long blonde hair belonged to a previous guest, maid, or maybe even a past female visitor.

Time quickly past and the wife was pushing the Department for them to close this rather high profile case. The official ruling on this case had to be made before the man's estate probate could even start to commence. Art could not tell the Captain that it was Bill who told him that the wife had actually been in that room. With only a suspicious wake-up call to go on; the Captain was definitely antsy and about ready to pull the plug on this entire affair. Art assured the Captain that Don's evidence would not only put the wife there in the room, but it would also show just what she had been doing there.

Bringing Don's name up at this point was crucial to this investigation. As it would appear that as part of the wife's long range strategy; she and her husband had made a rather large contribution to the Governor's reelection campaign. She had been married to this man for four years now and every single thing that she had done was directed towards this one event. Sure enough, the Governor himself had called Don, who pled with his uncle to allow the evidence to return from the lab.

Finally the results from the evidence came in from the lab, and now Art and Don were ready to spring their trap. The wife was called in and she just knew that she was there to hear that the case was now officially closed.

Art asked her, "Just why did your husband retire anyway?"

She responded, "I don't really know, possibly to spend more time with me."

"Yes," Art replied, "But that wouldn't leave him depressed, but possibly very satisfied I would say."

"I always tried to take very good care of my husband," she bragged.

"That's right," Art remarked, "all of his friends can definitely testify to that fact. But you say that your husband had become very depressed since retiring. Just why would that be?"

Now with the realization that they hadn't simply called her in to tell her the case was closed; she started choosing her words a lot more carefully, "I wouldn't actually say he was very depressed, but only somewhat."

Art looked right at her and asked, "Then what was it, greatly depressed or just somewhat?"

"Well he had started going off for days on end to places where he wouldn't usually go and without telling anyone where he was going," she replied.

"These places that you say he went off to, did you ever happen to go there yourself," Art asked?

She replied, "No, he never took me with him."

The wife was talking around the questions and wasn't actually answering Art's direct question; so he pushed her, "So you were never at any of these places?"

With this asked, she was now forced to outright lie to the men, while trying her best to talk around the answer to their questions, "No, he always went there alone and without telling anyone where he was going.

Art had already visited with the husband's long time confidante; who also just happened to be another woman. This woman had already laid everything out for him; so he knew exactly what had been going on. This particular woman and the husband had been friends ever since childhood; but had never once even thought of being more. It would seem that they basically knew too much about one another and didn't want to totally ruin a good friendship; that on top of the fact that this man was into women less than half his age. The husband had never even told his wife about this woman, but the wife had somehow found out about her. The wife felt that if things got really out of hand, she could always throw this would be girlfriend into the mix to confuse the matter even that much more. In fact, the man's wife had even worn a certain blonde wig on that particular night, just so that it would resemble her husband's friend's hair. Art was well aware that the wife was the one behind the man going off without telling anyone, to sleazy motels in other cities. The wife would then dress up as a low end hooker and would meet him there on the second night. He would then take his medication and this would allow the two of them to party all night long. Then when he was fast asleep, she would slip out of the room and leave just like a prostitute. He always had to leave five one hundred dollar bills on the dresser and she would also clean-out his billfold before leaving. This was the plan from the beginning and the man fairly well enjoyed this intrigue. However, this just left him penniless; so he actually kept his real billfold out in his car. Don had actually recovered both billfolds on that particular day; wondering just why that a man would need two billfolds. When the results from evidence finally made it in; they realized that the long blonde hair was probably from a wig that the wife had worn on that particular venture.

Art then asked the wife, "So just how long had it been since you and your husband had sex?"

Thinking quickly the wife said, "Just before he left out that day without telling anyone where he was going."

"That don't make any sense," Art remarked.

Quickly wanting to clarify what she had just said, "I was concerned that he might be going off to meet another woman; so I wanted him to be aware that she could in no way compete with me."

Art asked, "So you didn't ask him where he was going or even why that he was leaving out so secretly?"

"No, I just figured that it was his business and probably had something to do with his depression," she replied.

He had her going now; she was blaming another woman and depression for this man's death. Art broke it to her, "Are you aware that in his latest Will he leaves you nothing."

The true green eyed monster revealed itself at that time, "No, that's a lie, I had him wrapped tightly around my little finger and he wouldn't do anything like that. In fact he never did anything without consulting me first." Realizing just what she had said, she became very quiet and then finally asked, "Are you through with me or do I need to get an attorney."

Art looked over at Don and he was given the honors of arresting this very devious woman. They immediately left there and drove to Vicksburg; where they acquired a warrant to search the residence. Don took three blonde wigs as evidence and would now have to match that particular strand of hair to the wig from which it came. They also had impounded her car and Don thoroughly went through it looking for anything that might tie her to the crime scene. Art had told him about the parking lot being full and that the individuals were even having to park on the far side of the motel. This well known low end motel was visited by many of the working class and in particular day workers. These individuals weren't the most caring when it came time to throw things away; so a little bit of everything was all over the ground. Even one spraying contractor had leaked out a good bit of a particularly expensive herbicide and the chemical had pooled on the pavement in the back parking lot. When the next light rain came, the herbicide went all over the back parking lot. Don noticed a faint odor of this same chemical coming from the room's carpet, so he had it

analyzed. Sure enough it matched the particular
herbicide mixture that was all over the back side
parking area. Strangely enough this same herbicide
was also found on the carpet fibers of the wife's car.

When the news was aired that evening; they
showed a picture of the wife, told just what had
happened, when it happened, where it happened and
almost instantly received a call. A man who had
parked on the back side of the motel the night in
question; tried to pick up on a woman that he
perceived to be a hooker.

This woman had something on one of her shoes
and she was busy wiping it on the edge of the sidewalk
as he first approached her. She immediately told him
to get lost.

He asked her if his money wasn't just as good
and she replied, "Not for all the money in the world."
He told them that she looked like the woman he saw
on the news, but she had long blonde hair at that time.

Everything was coming together nicely by the
time of the pretrial bond hearing. Don was the one that
presented their evidence; with the blonde wig hair, her
bodily fluid mixed with the dead man's on the floor at
the side of the bed, her DNA on the toilet seat in the
restroom, and a very contradictory statement from her.
The Prosecutor painted a picture of a very cunning and
scheming woman, who had cleverly planned every
aspect of this man's death for over four years. The
Judge was not sympathetic towards her at all and set
her bail at one million dollars. With the new Will
purposely excluding her from everything; she would
have a hard time even raising a thousand dollars to bail
herself out with.

Later, on a plea bargain to take the death
penalty off the table, she opened up and told them
everything. As it turned out the wife had her husband

taking medication to enhance their love making. He had bragged to his female friend that his young wife could go on almost all evening long. She also had him taking vitamins, minerals, amino acid supplements, and Viagra; just so that he could stay up with her. He had suffered a long term heart condition and it had been her original intent to flat screw him to death. However, he was taking several medications for his heart and they were working way too well; at least as far as she was concerned. One of the man's heart medications contained a chemical known as Warfrin and it was used to thin an individual's blood. She studied up and learned just how dangerous that an accidental overdose of this medication could be and the plan was hatched. The evening in question, she had powdered several of his Warfrin pills and had replaced the contents of the amino acid capsule with the powdered Warfrin. Then she just applied a liberal dose of whiskey with his pills and went to work on him. This woman actually admitted that the sex that night was better than ever, as this whole situation had just super charged her. She never even stopped until he passed out.

Finished now she cleaned up any signs of her even being there, took the five one hundred dollar bills, left his billfold alone this time, opened his bottle of Warfrin and left. Hers would have been the perfect crime, if she just had not fallen prey to the team of Bill, Art and Don. In fact she had done her homework rather thoroughly and had learned that Morningwood presently had the lowest rate of case closures in the entire State of Mississippi. This due in no small part to the fact that the force was so under staffed, over worked, and fairly burned-out.

This time however, the Governor himself came and presented Art and Don with meritorious awards of excellence, in the service of the great State of Mississippi. By this time Don and Gina were getting a lot closer, and Art rather enjoyed having this extremely sharp young man around. In fact, he could easily get use to having him as a son-in-law.

Chapter Eight

Don asked, "Come on Art, I'm your partner. Just how was it that you knew all along that a woman had been in that man's room and that it was his wife?"

Art looked right at him and said, "I'm not lying, it was Bill, he told me."

Don just felt that this veteran officer was not interested in sharing his seemingly superior abilities, so he said nothing more. All along Don had felt uneasy in their taking a dog along on their cases, but he had to admit that Bill had not been any trouble at all.

As Art walked away he was saying loud enough for Don to hear, "I'm not lying, it was Bill, he told me everything."

With this last remark, Don felt that his partner was actually poking fun at him and was refusing to divulge where this amazing gut revelation had actually come from.

At the same time that they were working on this case, they had also been assigned twenty-six other cases. Some of them were way easier to close and Don's report writing ability was being taxed to the maximum. On this one particular case Bill had smelled cocaine, when none should have even been a consideration. Art had to carefully cover this revelation by saying that this whole situation reeked of drugs and most probably cocaine. Everyone, including Don, was simply appalled with this rather quick and brazen conclusion. Only when it was finally proved out to be true did anyone finally give in to Art's way of thinking. Art now knew better than to disagree with Bills super sensitive nose and it made him look more like an expert than he actually was. He would stick to the facts as Bill had provided them and then most of the evidence just backed up what he had previously told them. Art already knew that JW's abilities of deduction were phenomenal; but now with his superior sense of smell, he was absolutely amazing. Don was just not buying the fact that his partner had these super unreal abilities of deduction and came to him once more.

Art told him, "I don't know how to tell you more plainly; Bill has been the one giving me the information."

He heard Bill thinking, "Don't do it Art, no one will believe you and you'll just end up in the funny farm."

However, to the amazement of both of them, Don asked, "Alright, let's say that I want to believe you. How can you show me how this actually works?"

Thinking about it for a minute, Art said, "Tell him something simple that you want done. He can actually understand English."

Don really wasn't buying this as he asked Bill to go to his desk and bring him the letter opener. Bill immediately left and quickly showed up with Don's letter opener.

Not really knowing what to make of this, Don said, "Alright, I'll agree that he seems to somewhat understand what we say, but how does he tell you what he thinks or knows?"

Art replied, "Due to my head injury. After that I suddenly started hearing what Bill was thinking. I know that sounds absurd, but not nearly as absurd as what I'm about to tell you."

Totally caught off guard, Don just said, "Alright, I asked for it."

"The partner I had before had a phenomenal ability of deduction and I tried several times to figure him out without success. His name was JW and you can only imagine my surprise when Bill told me he was really JW; who had actually returned to help me out. I absolutely could not believe what he was saying, but he eventually proved it to me."

Don was just sitting there very quiet at this time and wasn't saying anything. Surely his wonderful partner hadn't lost it; but this revelation was absolutely far past being believable. With great hesitation, he asked, "How did he finally convince you that he was truly JW?"

Art, without any hesitation, replied, "It took a very long time and a lot of convincing before I finally gave in to the idea, but now I know he's right. In the future I'll relay you what Bill tells me and you can make up your own mind."

"On the Andrew's case you seemed to know that meth was involved from the very beginning. Are you telling me that Bill told you that he smelled meth there," Don asked?

"Yes, that's exactly what I've been trying to tell you," Art replied.

"Then tell me, just how is it that Bill knows just what meth smells like anyway," Don asked?

Art told Don about taking Bill down to the property room to smell the various drugs and how he actually discovered the problems with the property that he was smelling. Then he told of Bill hitting on the property room clerk; who just happened to be carrying some of those very drugs out of the evidence room at that exact moment. At this point Art told Don just what happened next.

"You mean you actually ended up killing a person based on what you were hearing from Bill," Don asked in a great state of absolute unbelief?

"Nothing strange about that, you killed someone based on what Bill was telling me. Remember when I looked back and told both of you to get ready; as it might get rather wild in there?"

Don thought about it for a minute and said, "I just figured that due to your police experience you felt uneasy about that situation."

"Alright," Art added. "I almost wish now that I had lied to you and told you that I just got all of this from superior intelligence, experience or maybe even a twisted gut feeling."

"No, never," Don remarked, "I do want to believe you, but you must admit that this has been a lot for me to process."

"I know," Art added, "Why don't we take Bill to one of those drug dog training sessions and I can show you what he can truly do."

Don spoke up, "Why don't we start with something a lot simpler. I'll hold up some fingers behind my back and Bill can tell you how many that I'm holding up."

Bill walked around behind Don and in no time at all Art said, "Three, but you're holding them down."

Don quickly ran his hand in his pocket, pulled out his change and bent over to show it to Bill. He asked Art, "How much money am I holding?"

Art spoke up, "Three quarters, two dimes, and four pennies."

Looking right at Bill, Don commented, "You really do understand everything, don't you?"

Bill simply shook his head up and down. Then Bill relayed to Art, "Don has been with a woman and I know who."

Art looked at Bill and said, "Some things we just need to keep to ourselves."

"Wait just one minute," Don remarked, "Aren't I your partner and didn't you tell me that you would relay to me anything that Bill told you."

"He just told me that you had been with a woman and he knew who," Art replied.

"Your exactly right Art, some things should just go unsaid." Don then looked over at Bill and said, "I can definitely see just how you could come in handy in our line of work."

"Yes," Art replied. "Like when he told me of the wife being in the motel with our suicide suspect."

"You were rather adamant about her guilt all along and I just was not for sure from the very start," Don remarked. Looking over at Bill he commented, "Shake your head up and down for yes and side to side for no. Are you really JW, and have you come back to help Art?"

Bill slowly shook his head up and down.

Don asked, "Are you really an angel in disguise?"

Bill slowly shook his head from side to side.

"Would you mind helping me out also," Don asked?

Bill just stood there and Art spoke up, "He doesn't know whether to shake his head up and down to let you know that he will help you also or side to side to indicated that he wouldn't mind helping."

Speaking up, Don remarked with a chuckle, "For a person with a legal degree, I'll have to be a lot more careful in the future with just how I phrase my questions."

With this Bill just shook his head up and down.

After the horrid run in with the neighbor's cat; Bill decided that he needed to be a lot smarter about how he handled him in the future. In fact the two of them had even came to a mutual agreement, where Bill had to show that he was keeping him out of the yard; but would not bother the cat outside the boundaries of the immediate yard. This worked rather well and they had even visited briefly from time to time concerning neighborhood issues. On this one particular night Bill caught a rather fat rat; which he heard coming in through the doggie door, to have his way in the house. Taking the rat outside, he tripped over to where the cat was hiding and promptly turned the rat over to him. As a goodwill offering in return; the cat told of an individual that had been slipping around the neighborhood at night and was looking in the windows. In fact the cat knew where this individual was located at that very moment. Bill didn't have to go far at all before he located the man and noticed him crawling in through a first floor rear window.

Quickly he headed for the house and directly into Art's bed room. In short order Art was up and shaking Don out. Of course he had to disregard the other person he saw there in Don's bed. They made a quick call for backup and headed off down the alley to the house in question. Slipping around the back of the house in the dark; they hid and waited on the officers to enter from the front. The officers quickly arrived, rang the door bell, and nothing happened. So at this point they started forcing the front door. At about this time an individual exited the back of the house through the back door and was looking straight down the barrel of Don's snub-nosed 38.

Don yelled, "Police, freeze."

The man totally disregarded this order and took off running. However, he didn't make it more than about ten feet before he found that he had a small dog with big teeth buried in the back of his right thigh. He was now dancing about, screaming something awful, hitting at Bill and his hand went to his waist band for a pistol. Before he could pull it though something came down hard on his head and he fell quickly to the ground. When he next looked up, he was looking straight down the barrel of Art's 45.

Art said calmly, "Move and I'll blow you're damn head off."

Don went over to Bill and was checking on him, "Are you alright, I'm sorry, but he totally disregarded my orders."The man might not have been in the house very long, but he was already in the process of violating the poor woman inside. Finally some of the officers made it around back and secured the prisoner.

As Art and Don were walking home, Art said, "Bill feels that you need to get rid of the toy gun and get a man stopper like I carry."

"Yes," Don replied, "but will the Captain allow me to carry a 45?"

"How can he possibly allow me to carry one and not you," Art added. "By the way, do we need to have a heart to heart talk on another matter?"

Don knew exactly what he was talking about and also knew that something had to be said. He spoke-up, "Art, I have to tell you that my intentions are nothing but honorable. I realize that this has been fairly quick, but things have moved along incredibly fast. I was in the process of looking for an apartment and now I feel that I will need a home."

Art knew exactly what he was saying. When Gina set her sights on him, he was a done deal, way before he even realized it. Art reached his hand out, took hold of Don's hand and said, "Welcome to the family son, I think my daughter made a wise choice, this time."

Don spoke-up, "Please don't say anything to her; I want everything to be at her time and choosing."

That next morning Art was sitting out on the deck with a cup of coffee when Gina came out. At first nothing was being said, then he asked, "Sleep well last night?"

"Like a baby, but I hear that you had some excitement thought," she replied.

Art was an ornery cuss, so he said, "Not much, just a man in a bed that he shouldn't have been in."

Looking straight at him, she remarked, "Don't worry, I have it all under control."

That next week they went shopping for a better gun for Don and the Captain gave them no problems at all in this matter. This night gave Don one more report to knock out and he was now even getting use to including Bill in their discussions. The Captain only whenced at the occasional mention of Bill's name; as he was merely waiting for that time when everything would go south with this whole situation. He couldn't believe how Don had fit right in with the team of Art and Bill. He had even talked to Don concerning Bill and this new young Detective was thrilled to be working with both Art and Bill.   In fact, unbeknownst to the Captain, Don had established a fair line of communication with Bill; where he interacted with head shakes, nods, tail wags, pawing, and growls. Art and Don had established new warning signals between the three of them and Bill's signal was his bark. In fact he was not to bark unless there was a situation at hand. This worked out rather well for all concerned. After a few weeks had gone by, Art asked Don, "Do you believe now that Bill is actually JW, my old partner, who has now come back as a dog?"

Don replied, "Yes I do, but let's just keep this between the two of us."

Art had been in contact with the drug task force and they were going to let him know when they were about to have their next drug-dog field-trials. If Bill could pass these trials, then he could be certified as an official drug detection dog. This would also make him a member of the force. Then there would be no question of him going with Art and Don on their calls. Art was so pleased with this situation that he even told the Captain and soon regretted this decision.

The Captain raised an eyebrow and told Art, "As long as the doctor figures that Bill being around is therapeutic for you, I will have little recourse except to allow him to go with you. However, if you want him along due to him being a trained canine; then he will also have to go through obedience and bite training."

Art now wished that he had not even brought this matter up and surely the Captain was well aware that no doctor had prescribed Bill as any type of therapy. He thought back to when he first told the Captain about Bill being a means of therapy for him and couldn't remember just what he had actually said at that time. The Captain on the other hand was not so naïve; but was willing to give this Bill situation a chance at bringing one of his best officers back to where he should be. In the mean time the Captain had grown to appreciate the things that this small dog had done and wished that all of his officers had a small partner such as Bill. He really actually wasn't putting it on Art when he mentioned the obedience and bite training; as he had become fairly concerned with Bill's biting people. No, he had not bitten anyone that didn't need it, but possibly that might just happen next. Sitting down with Don and Bill, Art explained just what had happened and all three were now ready for the additional training that Bill would have to go through.

Chapter Nine

Just about one month later the obedience training was slated to start. Our trio showed up that morning along with several of the other dogs and their handlers. The instructor started laying out just what all they planned on accomplishing in the next few weeks and even had one of their trained dogs run through his paces. Art, Don and Bill watched this closely and pretty well knew that Bill could already do everything that was going to be expected of him. Art also realized that they couldn't take that much time away from working the streets, just to complete this extensive course.

The trio was looking around the room and most of the other dogs were more interested in smelling each other's butts than what was being presented by the instructor. The instructor told everyone that the first step was to catch their dog's attention and then they could move on from there. He said that a well trained dog had his mind constantly focused and his eyes were for his handler only.

When the instructors talk was over he let everyone go for the day, but told them to be back there promptly at eight in the morning. Art approached the instructor and asked, "We have already paid our fee in full, but were just wondering if we could challenge the final test to see if we could test out of the program?"

The instructor had never had anyone come forward with such a request before and said, "That's an odd request; but I don't really think that it would be unreasonable. Many people have well trained dogs, but we have never seen any that were so trained that they could pass our final obedience test."

They proceeded to the test field and the instructor started telling Art just what he wanted his dog to do. The instructor actually felt that this could be amusing to watch. Art's only part was in repeating what Bill had already heard first hand from the instructor.

They started down through the various tasks and at one point the instructor stopped and asked Art, "Is this some sort of trick, this dog has already been through obedience training. I hope you are not going to ask for your money back, as there are no refunds."

Art replied, "No, it's not a trick, the Captain requested that we bring him down here for obedience training. I honestly didn't believe he needed it; as he is extremely smart. But we do need a piece of paper from you stating that he has passed his obedience training."

The instructor continued on and in about thirty minutes called everything to a halt. He exclaimed, "It would be my distinct pleasure to declare this dog as being obedience trained."

With the first leg of Bill's training now behind them; that following week they took Bill down to the drug detection trials. They watched as several dogs requalified and Art once more talked with the instructor. He was not at all amenable to the testing of a dog that had not come through a certified training school. Art asked him if he was a betting man; as he pulled out five one-hundred dollar bills.

The man looked right at Art and said, "You cannot bribe me or buy your dog a certification."

"No, you have it all wrong," Art added. "I just want to bet you that my dog can tell the difference between cocaine, marijuana, heroine, and meth. You hide all four and I'll have him go find whichever one you want him to find."

He looked at Art for the longest and then said, "Let's see if I understand you right. I get the money if he doesn't find the one I ask for; but what if he does find the right one by accident?"

Art exclaimed, "I'll send him out four times and you tell me which one you want him to find each time."

In utter amazement, the man asked, "But just what do you get out of this in return?"

"My dog's certification, if he can do this one thing that none of your dogs could even hope to do," Art replied.

"Alright, I'll take that bet," the man exclaimed!

The man went off to hide the simulated drugs and Don asked, "Isn't that asking a lot of Bill?"

"Well it appears that this is the only chance Bill will have at getting certified," Art replied. "Besides, it was actually Bill's idea."

The instructor came back and asked, "Well, is your dog ready?"

Art replied, "Bill is always ready."

The instructor leaned over to Art and whispered, "Tell him to find the marijuana."

Art looked right at Bill and said, "Marijuana Bill, find the marijuana."

Bill took off at a dead run and circled the inside of the building where the drugs were supposedly hidden. Then he went over to a pile of old oily rags and barked. When Art, Don and the instructor showed up; Bill started pawing at a certain place in the pile. The instructor reached down, picked up some of the rags, and there lying below was the pouch marked marijuana.

He looked over at Bill and said, "Tell him to find the cocaine."

Bill was very careful not to do anything until Art gave him the command. Then he took off and found the cocaine pouch taped to the bottom of an old chair, which was in a rack with several other old chairs.

Once again the instructor said, "Tell him to go find the methamphetamine."

Art said, "Meth Bill, find the meth."

Bill took off and circled the area. Then he went out to the center of the building and simply started looking everything over. Finally he started jumping straight up in the air; as the packet had been pulled up on a string, almost to the ceiling.

By now the instructor knew that there was no chance at getting his hands on all that money, so he said, "If he finds the heroin packet, I'll be glad to give him a drug detection certification."

Bill didn't even wait for Art's command, but rather took off at a dead run and went straight out of the building. All three men were surprised and followed after him. When they came out of the building, Bill was barking something fierce and jumping up on the side of the instructor's truck.

Art was very much surprised to hear Bill thinking loudly, "The heroin packet was never actually taken out of the truck."

Art looked over at the instructor strangely and asked, "Just why didn't you hide the heroin packet like the others?"

The instructor, spoke-up, "I really didn't think that your little dog would actually get that far. Then if he did by some miracle, I wanted to see how he would handle being sent out for drugs that weren't actually there. It's not enough for you to know your dog can find drugs, but you also need to know how he will react to drugs not being there."

Art asked, "Well how about his certification?"

"He found the heroin, didn't he," the man remarked while looking down at Bill in amazement. "If you should ever decide that you might want to sell him, I'll give you top dollar. In fact, I feel that you should know that a dog like yours would be worth well over twenty thousand dollars down on the border."

Art just smiled and replied, "We'll keep that in mind."

Bite training was the only thing remaining and Art had a terrible time even finding an instructor. No matter how smart Art told the man Bill was; the instructor insisted that biting only on command didn't come natural for a dog. They finally came to an agreement, where that Art and Bill could attend one of their trainings. The instructor was amused that a Detective would even want a bite trained Jack Russell Terrier; so he allowed the two of them to come see just what would be expected of a bite trained dog. This training was not even held in Mississippi; so our three crime fighters had to take a couple of days off just to attend to this training. When that day finally rolled around; Art, Don and Bill showed up and all were immediately intimidated. There were several large dogs there of various breeds, with each and every one specifically trained to bite. These dogs would lie patiently at their master's side and watched closely as the man in the bite suit took off. Each was waiting for their own separate command to attack. The biggest thing was that these dogs went for the arms and their body mass was heavy enough to drag the man down to the ground. Each dog in turn would latch on tightly and wouldn't release until given the command to do so. Finally at the end of the day, as almost a joke, the instructor asked Art if he would like to give his smart dog a try. By this time the man in the heavy bite suit was fairly worn out and was totally ready for this whole thing to be over. However, he was given the signal once more to run out and Art finally gave Bill the command to attack. Bill seemed way faster than the other dogs at getting to the man and that was when they got to see just how smart he truly was. Normally the man would face the attacking dog and take on the full force of the bite. However, Bill got there incredibly fast and just started circling the man. The man in the bite suit was not totally covered in the back and was afraid that this small dog would bite him from behind. They went around and around until the man was fairly dizzy and then Bill hit him on the arm and clamped down hard. The very tired man was now thoroughly dizzy, still going around and the additional weight on his arm took him straight to the ground. Needless to say, there were some serious negotiations that went on at that time; but Bill at least left there a certified attack dog.

Bill's three certifications proudly hung on Art and Don's short cubical wall, along with a rather cute picture of Bill and Teddy. Needless to say this did nothing to improve the atmosphere around the Department. It would seem that the only one slightly impressed was the Captain. Don and Art continued to take Bill with them to their crime scenes; but now, in writing at least, Bill was allowed to interact a lot more with both men.

At one particular crime scene, Bill barked and Don was the only one around. He left what he was doing and went over to where Bill was located.

Don asked, "What is it Bill, drugs?"

Bill simply shook his head back and forth and pawed at a spot on the carpet.

Don got down on his hands and knees and didn't see anything. He looked back at Bill and said, "What is it Bill, body fluids?"

Once more Bill shook his head back and forth and pawed again at the same spot on the carpet.

Don went after his flash light, kneeled down really close to the spot and meticulously searched through the heavy carpet fibers. Then all of a sudden he saw a glint and noticed a small diamond laying there on the floor. Someone had evidently lost this diamond from a ring or something of the such. The stone wasn't very large and possibly could have belonged to anyone else that had ever been in that particular room. Don appreciated Bill's help with this, but didn't really put much importance into the finding of that diamond. Later when Art showed up, Don learned through Art that the owner of that particular diamond had been in the room with the man who was now dead.

Art had learned from talking with everyone in the adjoining apartments, that the dead man was actually a transvestite, who openly desired to be a woman. This was just confirmed by looking around the apartment; as ninety percent of the clothes in there belonged to a woman of Sam's size. His or her name had actually been legally changed to Samantha Finley and this individual went by the name of Sam. Bill didn't hit on any drugs being present, but did smell a considerable amount of stale cigarette smoke and alcohol. He also had relayed to Art that the man who had lost the diamond was probably a smoker and possibly a trucker. The trucker part Bill picked up on from the fresh odor of diesel that was on one of the chairs near the bed.

After finishing with the crime scene and armed with all of this additional information, Art and Don started canvassing the dives or bars near the truck stops. They had a picture of Sam and several of the bar managers recognized Sam as a local prostitute that frequented their establishments. However, none of them remembered seeing her in the last week or two. Finally at one of the truck stops, a woman remembered seeing Sam about three days before; which would have been about the time that she/he had been killed. Talking with everyone around there, they learned where that Sam hung out with some of the other prostitutes and some of them may have seen something. As fortune would have it, a man had approached Sam and one of the other prostitutes at the same time. He looked both of them over and decided on Sam. The woman watched as Sam climbed up into his rather large silver diesel pickup truck and they drove away. She also noticed that it had a different tag than Mississippi and rather large tires. The man she described was of average build; wore a dirty pullover T-shirt, jeans, and boots. Upon looking through the book of all the State tags, she felt that the tag might have been from South Carolina.

While writing the reports up on this incident, Don once more had to make Art out to be an absolute genius at reading crime scenes. Bill had been the one to do the work; but nothing could be said about the dog discovering the diamond, smelling a man there, the odor of cigarettes, or the fresh smell of diesel. Even though Bill was invaluable to their investigations, nothing much could be mentioned about most of his involvement.

However, this was one case that the three super sleuths could not quickly put to rest; try as they might. In fact this case just added to their statistics of unsolved cases.

One thing of direct benefit on the unsolved cases was Bill's ability to sniff the evidence at anytime. In this manner they could refresh his memory as they came across additional information leading to new suspects.

At about this time, animosity within the Department was at an all time high; due to Art and Don having an above sixty percent closure rate. In fact they had now moved to the top of the roster. Which meant that they were next in line for the next new unit arriving; whenever that should be. Whenever new vehicles were purchased for the department, the new ones went to the Cities best and finest; leaving everyone else to fall in line for which ever hand me down was being given up. Detectives Roberts and Wagner had received these new units ever since Art and JW's fall from glory, with a closure rating of less than thirty-five percent. However, thirty-five percent just wasn't going to cut it this year. Actually Wagner was a pig and he was always eating something; as a result any vehicle that they passed down definitely needed a very through fumigating. Most of the time he didn't even get to finish what he was eating there at his desk, as it seemed as if their phone was always ringing. In fact it rang more than almost all the other detectives there in the Department put together. Not many knew that these two men were also acting as realtors on some of the cities low end properties. This situation actually worked out rather well for the realty company; as not many of their realtors would go into those parts of the City. If anyone should ever enquire into Robert or Wagner's whereabouts, they were always following up on their cases in those areas of the City. Amazingly so, their constant presence in those areas did help them form a rapport with the locals; which gave them information to close several of their cases.

Wagner was not one to be picky and often he
would hours later finish a candy bar or doughnut left
on his desk from earlier that morning. Once he came in
to find Bill standing on his desk. Bill was actually
scanning through the documents laying face-up on the
desk; but Wagner thought that he was up there for
what remained of a cheeseburger from the day before.
He hollered at Bill, calling him, "That damn dog," then
went in and made a spectacle out of jumping down
Art's throat. If that wasn't bad enough, he even went
in and made a formal complaint to the Captain. The
Captain was smarter than this and knew where all the
anger was coming from; but told Wagner that he
would write-up the dog. Both Roberts and Wagner felt
that they were onto something here and purposely left
food lying around on their respective desks after that.
Two other Detectives, Russell and Baines, watched this
whole affair unfold and felt that they could only better
themselves by playing one side against the other.
However, there was one other who had watched and
heard everything that was being plotted, Bill. He
thought this whole matter to be comical and even told
Art what all had been going on. Baines would walk by
Wagner's desk when he was out and would purposely
eat anything he saw laying there. Wagner would then
come in and complain to the Captain that the damn
dog was back at it again, and his write-ups were
worthless. Coming to Art, the Captain would only
hear that it wasn't Bill and that they had no real proof.
This situation set the stage for a potential catastrophe.
One morning Art, Don and Bill came in as usual; but
Bill hit on something that had happened there during
the night. What he noticed was rat pellets and they led
across the floor to the file room. This hadn't always
been a file room, but once was a washroom. As a result
there were holes in the walls which no one felt the need

in closing off. Immediately below one of these holes lay the somewhat large and very dead the rat that Bill had been tracking through the squad room. Bill noticed how it looked as if the rat could not control its bowel movements and felt that this rat had been poisoned. The rat pellet trail began at Wagner's desk and Bill felt that Wagner was most likely the one who had done this. He immediately went over to Art and told him of the entire situation. Art at this point was thoroughly put out with the fact that Wagner would actually try to hurt his dog. He went to the Captain and insisted that he follow him into the squad room. There were still several crumbs of a piece of chocolate cake on the corner of Wagner's desk. As Art and the Captain approached, Wagner quickly tried to wipe them onto the floor. This just made the situation that much better; as he had actually wiped them onto the rat pellets on the floor below. Art showed the Captain the cake crumbs and the rat pellet trail leading away from Wagner's desk. Then he insisted that the Captain follow him into the file room, to where he showed him the dead rat.

With this Art accused Wagner to his face of trying to poison Bill. Wagner got really mad and even wanted to get up and settle this entire matter right then and there.

Art said, "You stupid fool, Baines has been the one eating everything off of your desk. He's just been playing you as the fool you really are."

Wagner turned pale and so did the Captain; as Baines had called in sick that very morning. In fact his wife was the one who had actually called and said that they were rushing him to the emergency room.

Quickly the Captain spoke-up, "Wagner, you better come clean and I mean right now.

Wagner was now afraid and didn't quite know exactly what to admit to.

The Captain quickly added, "Wagner, you fool, we're going to get that rat tested and if you have poisoned Baines, you just better hope that he doesn't die."

Wagner was now very nervous, as he said, "I didn't mean to hurt anyone; I was just tired of that dog getting everything he wants."

The Captain came back, "You get on the phone right now and call the hospital. The doctor will need to know what Baines ate."

A good while later, when Baines finally came back to work, the Captain came in and said, "From this day forward there will be no more food brought into this squad room. I expect for all of you to get along and if you can't, possibly you need to be looking for something else where you can."

It was just about this time when Art got a hit on his inquiry into other similar hate crimes involving homosexuals or transvestites. The location was Memphis, Tennessee and they had a dead man that had just stabbed a homosexual to death. Yes, a dead man, who was very much alive as he tried to run from the scene, with the knife still in his hand, and ran straight into a rookie officer who put one fatal shot dead center. However, this man was not driving a silver colored diesel pickup truck and was a little shorter than what they would have considered as being average.

Art asked, "Does he possibly have a ring that is missing a diamond."

The Detective from Memphis replied, "No, but he used some sort of ceremonial knife on his victim and it's missing a stone."

One fairly quick road trip to Memphis and Bill confirmed that it had been this man's odor which was in Sam's room. Don collected some DNA and finally with these results in hand, the confirmation was made to this killer. Once more, the now notorious trio had leaped tall buildings at a single bound, closing one more additional case."

Chapter Ten

By this time Don had been living at Art's home
for almost a year and nothing was basically being said;
as everyone there was well pleased with this situation.
All were very aware that Gina was the main hold-up in
their getting married. She just didn't put much faith in
that particular legal contract; as that was the point from
which her first marriage had started straight down hill.
Don however was not her first husband, was nothing
like him and she knew that very well. Art on the other
hand was extremely satisfied with his young partner
and wouldn't trade him for any of the other Detectives,
even if he could. Sue Ann already looked at him as her
son-in-law and had actually introduced him as such to
several of her very close friends. This was the situation
as it stood on the morning that Art and Don were
dispatched to one of the high end hotels there in
Morningwood.

When they arrived; the hotel staff directed them
to room 314 and unlocked the door for them. They
learned that one of the maids had already opened the
door, but quickly shut it without going in.

The manager just looked down at Bill and asked,
"He is house-broke, isn't he?"

Don replied, "No worries mate."

Then the manager wanted to know if they could
take the body down the back stairs, as not to startle any
of the guests.

Art told him, "When the Medical Examiner
shows up you can discuss that with him."

Easing into the room, Bill started sniffing and Art heard, "Three different men were here, one black and the dead girl."

Laying there sprawled across the bed, sparsely clothed, was a very pretty black girl and there was little doubt that she had been shot twice in the upper torso. The medical examiner decided that the time of death was approximately fifteen hours ago. The room had been registered to the dead girl, Troyla Rosemont, and she had informed the hotel that it was just for one person. Troyla had been raised there in Morningwood and was suppose to be off at college, or at least she was registered at that time at Ole Miss.

Examining the bed it was fairly evident that someone had enjoyed sex there. Bill needed only a few sniffs to reveal that Troyla and the black man were the ones who actually had sex there on the bed.

Forwarding Bill's findings on to Don, Art made light of this situation by saying, "What were the two white men doing, watching?"

Bill was still working his nose and centered in on the dead girls fingers. He let Art know in short order that she had the smell of one of the white men on her right hand. Don swabbed her hands for DNA evidence and collected fingernail scrapings. Neither of the slugs had passed through her body, so they would definitely have bullet evidence.

Don collected body fluids and hairs from a black individual on the sheets of the bed. Bill discovered that someone had done a line of coke on the bedside table. He looked at Troyla's nose and saw the tale tell signs of extended cocaine usage. One sniff was enough to confirm that she was the one who had probably done this line of coke.

But just who had brought the drugs to this room? Most likely the black man had brought the coke and as a result ended up enjoying sex with her.

Don was in the process of collecting a sample of wine from a broken wine glass. This particular glass had been thrown against the far wall. He asked, "Do you think that she could have been a high-end hooker?"

Art replied, "Could be, but something is just not right about this situation. What exactly were the two white men doing here and how did the girl end up with one of their odors under her fingernails?"

Collecting the remainder of the evidence, they found no shell casings and assumed that the killer had used a revolver. Such was the extent of the evidence collected that day and the body was released to the Medical Examiner; who promptly took it down using the elevator. None of the guests that had been registered at the time of her death, on that floor, were still there. This meant that a lot of phone calls would have to be made and a lot of people would have to be run down for statements.

Visiting with Troyla's mother; she really didn't act as if this surprised her much, but she wouldn't exactly elaborate on why. She only allowed that her overly beautiful daughter was about to be married to an influential Mississippi Senator's son. Everyone knew Senator Clarence Whitney and what they knew was that he was truly at the seat of power in Mississippi.

Don, spoke-up, "Possibly I should call the Senator before the girl's death comes out on the evening news."

Art asked, "Do you know the Senator?"

"Yes, his family and mine go way back and I've even spent time at their beach home,"

Don remarked.

"You are aware that his son could be a potential suspect, if he caught his fiancée here with another man," Art remarked?

Don quickly spoke-up, "Please let me handle that situation; as it could get rather touchy."

Don called the Captain and filled him in on this whole situation. He informed the Captain that he was headed up to Jackson, where the Senator lived, so he could visit face to face with him. That next morning Art found that he was almost at a loss, as Don had done all of their reports over this last year. He was egger to jump right in and get started, but definitely wanted this report to sound just as professional as their previous ones. So Art just decided to make notes on everything they now knew, instead of generating any reports. Quickly he discovered that without the information furnished by Bill, they practically had nothing. Well maybe not exactly nothing, as they did have the evidence gathered by Don. Mostly Bill and Art just killed time for the better part of that day, and then went out to follow up on some of their other cases. All day long Art waited to hear from Don, but he heard nothing. This really started to wear on Art and it gave him cause for concern. Possibly he should have insisted on going with his young partner; as he definitely had more experience in questioning suspects. He waited all evening to hear from Don, but still nothing was forthcoming. That next morning he checked to see if Don had made it in during the night but he hadn't. Showing up for work, Art found that Don had already completed the report on this case. It was rather short and to the point; nothing at all like Don's previous reports.

Art asked his partner, "Did you learn something that no one should know?"

Don immediately became very defensive, "Art, without the information that we learned from Bill, we basically have nothing."

"We have the evidence that you collected," Art replied.

"Yes that," Don remarked, "I just don't know how but I believe that we must have left some of it at the crime scene, as I just can't seem find it."

Art looked right at Don and said, "You know something and you're trying to cover this entire affair up for the Senator, aren't you?"

Don remarked, "Art, just let this one go, there are several cases out there that we have failed to close and this one needs to be one of those."

"Well I never," Art replied, "You're throwing everything that we worked so hard for away for a no good for nothing killer. You may be through with this one; but I don't have to put my tail between my legs, just to run and hide. I'm going to stick with this case and I will close it."

Art took off and was furious with his would be partner. Just when he needed him; his blue blood came out and ruined everything. He now thought that surely Don would make a wonderful politician in the future; because he definitely was not to be trusted. Art went home that day and let everyone know just what type of person Don had truly turned out to be. Gina almost instantly started bawling and took off for her room. Bill was throwing his two cents worth in and he definitely agreed with Art. That evening no one even saw Don, as he didn't show up at the house once again. Several beers later, Art and Bill were both convinced that they didn't really need Don and had done rather well for themselves without him. The following morning Art went in to work with a strong resolve to dig into this matter and get to the bottom of just who had killed this young girl.

While Art was at work, Don came by the house and picked up his belongings.

Gina refused to even speak with him and only Sue Ann was somewhat calm at this time.

She asked, "Isn't there some way that the two of you can work through this matter?"

Don replied, "I sure wish there was, but I feel that Art will hate me for a very long time. I do want you to know however that what I did was for the both of us, not just me."

Art walked in at work that same morning and the entire squad room was set-up as some very huge party. Everyone except for Don was there and the Mayor, Police Chief and News Medias were in attendance. When they saw him everyone started in with a round of, "For he's a Jolly Good Fellow." Then the Mayor spoke-up and announced to everyone; that the City was recognizing the lifelong exemplary work that Art had performed for this City over these many years. In fact, they were as of today giving him full early retirement and a year's salary as a bonus to go with that. Art was speechless, as this would have been a wonderful gesture if it weren't for the fact that they were purposely killing his ability to follow-up on this case and he was well aware it.

He asked, "Who will follow-up on my cases?"

The Captain remarked, "You just don't worry about that, I've already assigned them to Russell and Baines."

Art knew that these two had the absolute worst case closure record of anyone in the Department and with this all of his cases were now dead.

At one point he got Baines aside and asked, "Have you even looked at the case involving Troyla Rosemont?"

Baines told him, "No need, Don has already closed that case and we're going to make an arrest as soon as we locate him."

"Arrest who," Art asked?

"Her boyfriend, Tremain Walker," Baines remarked.

Art was now doubly upset; as he had been left totally out of this situation and had not even been allowed to talk with the high and mighty Senator Whitney. The Police Chief came up and asked Art for his badge; as they were going to have it framed to hang there in the squad room. Art had nothing more left for this place; so he just turned and walked out the door. When he got home he learned that Don had already been there and gone. In one sense he was relieved that he wouldn't have to see his face again, but then he would like to question him about Tremain Walker. Sue Ann was ecstatic about Art being retired and the huge bonus that he had received. She told him of Don saying that he did this for the both of them and Art just took a beer from the fridge.

Three weeks later Art was still taking beers from the fridge and Sue Ann was really starting to worry. Bill would sit there and try to talk with him, but Art just wouldn't speak with him. The more depressed that Art became the more Gina totally blamed Don for everything. He had tried to call and speak with her, but she refused to even speak with him.

Then the other shoe fell; as it made the headlines of the local paper that Tremain Walker had been charged with the murder of Troyla Rosemont and Donald Claybourn had been promoted to the position of Assistant Police Chief. Art and the rest of the family

could not believe this turn of events; but secretly Sue
Ann had been visiting with Don and had even
congratulated him on his accomplishment.

Art was out in his usual chair with a beer and
Bill was lying right there next to him when the door
bell rang. Sue Ann was the only one that would go to
the door, so she looked out the window. There in front
of their house was a huge car with a driver standing
beside it. She opened the door and definitely
recognized the man standing there to be Senator
Whitney.

He asked, "Is Art here?" She shook her head up
and down and he asked, "Do you think that he would
speak with me?"

Opening the door further, she motioned for him
to come in. By this time she finally was able to speak
and said, "He's out in the back yard, please come this
way."

They went out to where Art was sitting and the
Senator walked around in front of Art. He asked, "Do
you know who I am?"

Art only mumbled, "Who doesn't."

"May I sit down and speak with you," he asked?

Motioning towards a chair Art looked up at Sue
Ann and asked, "Sugar, would you mind getting us a
couple beers?"

Art sincerely wanted to hear just what this man
had to say, that had now utterly destroyed so many
lives.

When the Senator started in he made no
apologies for anything; but in true form started in with
his problems rather than Art's. "I feel that I need to tell
you all about the situation which led up to this all
happening." He only stopped once and that was to
stand and thank Sue Ann for the cold beer. "I only
have the one child and have always tried to do right by

him. All of his life I have given him everything that he
ever wanted; and he has done nothing but rebel against
everything that I stand for and believe in. Still he is my
only child and I would do anything for him. He is very
much of this present age, and views Mississippi in a
totally different light than I do. I'm still not liberal
enough to be overly pleased with the mixed marriages
that we see daily out on our streets. However, Daniel
sees nothing wrong with this and even brought home a
very lovely colored girlfriend. Then he broke it to us
that he and Troyla Rosemont were to be married. As
much as I disagreed with this situation, I gave my
blessings. Troyla was one of the most beautiful young
women that I had ever laid eyes upon; and at least in
Daniel's presence, she was so sweet that sugar
wouldn't melt in her mouth. The two of them were
only at the house that one time for three days and I
thought that I could definitely grow to like this colored
girl. Away from their presence, my wife and I would
talk. It had always been our hearts desire to see our
son go into politics and possibly even run for Governor
some day. With a beautiful colored wife and his good
name, he might have just what he needed to easily
occupy the Governor's Mansion. By the time that they
left that weekend; my wife and I had probably
experienced every emotion possible or so we thought.
However, that following week I was back in my office
at the Capitol and who should walk in but Troyla. I
got up from my chair and came to greet her. When we
got close I felt that she wanted a hug instead of a hand
shake. You know how it is with some women;
sometimes they would rather a good hug. I reached
out my arms to hug her and she came straight in and
gave me a kiss. Not one of those little pecks on the
mouth, but rather a hard kiss. I pushed her away and
she acted as if she was offended. Then she started in

and told me that she saw how I had been looking at her back there at the house. Caught totally by surprise, I told her that I was simply admiring her beauty. She quickly explained that she went for the older type and wouldn't mind getting something going with me. No matter what that woman looked like, I definitely wouldn't do anything like that to my son and told her so. That was when she came straight with me and told me that she wasn't interested in my son; but rather my money. I asked her how much it would cost for her to totally leave him alone. She looked right at me and told me that she knew I was worth well over forty million. That girl had done her homework and I now saw her true nature. Then she informed me that she was giving me a bargain today; my son back for a mere five million dollars. I couldn't believe what I was hearing and just stood there with my mouth wide open. Troyla told me to meet her there at the hotel, where you found her, at exactly six o'clock with the money. Once she left I started thinking this entire mess over and came to the conclusion that I wanted to pay her to leave my son alone. However, I had always been a cheapskate and just figured that one million in cash would definitely do the trick. Heading over here that day, I timed it to where I would arrive at exactly six o'clock. I was carrying the brief-case with the one million in it when I found the door to the room slightly ajar. There lying on a totally messed-up bed was Troyla and it was very apparent that she had just been enjoying a very aggressive bout of sexual activity. She was totally nude and didn't try in the least to hide herself from my view. Crawling down to my end of the bed she asked if I liked anything that I saw. Quickly changing the conversation; I opened the brief-case and showed her the money. Troyla told me that it didn't look like five million to her and I told her it was only one million, take it or leave it. She rolled over on her back, spread her legs and just laughed at me. I closed the brief-case and said that it was one million or nothing. Troyla put a hand down between her legs and told me that it was worth forty-million and all she had to do was marry young Daniel. At this point I quickly left the room and didn't see her again. After I heard that she had died, I started a trust fund so that all of her brothers and sisters could go off to school and put the one million dollars in that fund."

All this time Bill had been telling Art that the smell under Troyla's finger nails had been from the Senator.

Art spoke-up, "Sounds like a good story Senator; but how do you explain your skin being under her fingernails and where did those scratches on the side of your face come from anyway?"

"You truly are as good as I thought you were and I shouldn't have glazed over things so fast," he remarked. "When I came into the room; Troyla totally naked came clean out of the bed and attacked me. When I pushed her away, she clawed the side of my face. I threw the brief-case over on the bed and she was the one that opened it. She realized that it was short a few million and threw her fit. Everything else is just as I told you."

"So just how did the police come up with the fact that Tremain Walker killed Troyla and what about your son," Art asked?

The Senator spoke-up, "I don't know anything about the police's case against Mr. Walker; and I can assure you that my son had nothing to do with any of this."

"I understand that she was killed with a 38. You don't happen to own one, do you," Art asked?

"I did," remarked the Senator, "but it mysteriously came up missing the very weekend that Troyla came home with my son. I wouldn't be in the least surprised if she didn't steal it from my study."

"One last question Senator, "Just why is it that you're at my home today anyway?"

"Because I have hurt some people in this matter and really never meant to," he replied. With this, the Senator got up and said, "Just stay where you are, I'll show myself out."

The Senator was no more than out of sight when the conversation between Art and Bill got in-depth. This was one situation where they both were definitely not in agreement. Art felt that the Senator was just covering up for his son and Bill felt that he had told the entire truth. Sue Ann was watching from the open kitchen window and was definitely worried about Art's sanity. In a few minutes Bill came in as he felt that Art was definitely being pig headed about this entire matter. After all, he had always been a better judge of character than Art. Bill came in to where Sue Ann was and just looked up at her for the longest. He wished that he could at least talk with her about Art's situation.

Sue Ann spoke-up, "Don't look at me; he talks with you a lot more than he does me."

Chapter Eleven

Throughout this entire ordeal Gina's closest confidant was also her best friend, Lisa May Broadmore. These two women had been through a lot together and had kept their sanity by sharing every single thought with each other. Both of them had failed marriages and children to take care of, but Lisa had an education to fall back on. Even before her divorce she had been smart enough to get out and get herself a job. After two major job changes, she at present had been working for the Mayor's Office for the last two years. She was well aware of how much Gina hated what Don had done to her father; but she also knew just how much Gina truly loved and missed him. She tried to talk some sense into her friend, but Gina was just as bull headed as her father. With both Art and Sue Ann now at home to watch Teddy, Gina felt that it might be a good time to start searching for a job. Up to this point she had been a stay at home mom and really didn't have a lot of qualifications to draw from. However, if they were ever looking for the most personable individual around, she was fully qualified.

Lisa called Gina one day and said, "Gina you're just not going to believe it. The Mayor's office is looking for an individual to work as a public liaison; to coordinate between the various departments. I mentioned your name and they're very interested in talking with you."

Gina asked with a real depressed tone of voice, "They'll have to go through the regular hiring process won't they?"

"No," Lisa remarked, "it's only a temporary position, but possibly they may make it a full time job later, if certain things work out."

Gina showed up at the Mayor's Office for her interview and the heads of all the various departments were present. However, Don was there representing the Police Department. One of the questions asked by the Mayor himself was whether she would have problems working with Don. Gina replied that she would have no problem at all working with Don. All of the department heads gave their approval and Gina was officially employed. Don was very pleased; as now Gina would have to listen to everything he had to say and he just needed to wait for the right moment.

It was at this time and out of nowhere that Senator Whitney was found shot to death at his home. The official ruling was suicide; being that he left a note and had even purchased the very gun that morning. Don asked the officials if he could assist with the case and they were more than willing to accommodate his request; as the Senator had also confessed to killing Troyla Rosemont in his suicide note. During the investigation, the one thing that no one had an answer for was the blob of plastic; which had melted down in a small fire right there on the Senator's desk. The blob was scraped up and sent off for possible analysis. Don was not one to miss an opportunity and inquired into who would fill the unexpired term of the Senator. It was not unheard of for the wife or even a very close friend of the family to be put forth for possible Senate approval, as a short term replacement. He spoke openly with the Senator's wife and she made only one demand of him, if he was interested in getting her vocal support. That demand was for him to get to the bottom of this entire matter and totally clear her husband's name. Don told her that he would have to question her son and she just asked if she could sit in on the questioning. This was a very unusual request, due to the son's age; but with his mother's assurance that she would not utter one single word, Don agreed. He knew that she definitely had the need to know just exactly what her son was actually going to say. After speaking with the son, the entire picture became very clear and he knew that he had some good old fashioned police work that needed to be done. Even before speaking with the son, Don knew that they had arrested the right man to start with, but he needed proof that this man had also somehow caused the Senator's death.

Back at Art's place, "I told you so," was the theme of the day; with the Senator's written confession publicized all over the various news Medias. Bill was just not going to stand for the nose rubbing that Art was handing out, so he headed for the house. Once in the house he went in to where Sue Ann was sitting and hopped right up in her lap. She knew that he and Art were not getting along for some reason; as Bill very seldom came to her.

Art came in to where they were and uttered, "I told you so."

Sue Ann, spoke-up, "Alright Art, that's just about enough. I'm thoroughly fed up with all this nonsense. I know that you came in here just to say that to the dog. We haven't had a decent conversation since this whole mess started and I'm getting pretty tired of you talking to the dog."

This caught Art totally by surprise; as he thought he had been fairly careful not to speak openly with Bill, except when no one was around. However, his beer drinking had caused him to lower his guard and Sue Ann had witnessed him speaking to Bill on several occasions. She was afraid of what was happening to him and didn't know if the alcohol or psycho-ward would get him first. Sue Ann had dreamed of Art being retired; but it definitely didn't look anything like the reality that she was now living.

Art looked down at Bill and said, "It's time that we fill her in on this whole matter; but you might want to get down from her lap before I tell her."

Sue Ann was about to cry; as it seemed as if nothing she had just said had soaked into Art's thick head at all. Bill jumped down and went over by Art.

Art sat down next to Sue Ann and took hold of her hand. "I'm not crazy, but I want you to hear me out completely before you pass judgment."

She was very quiet and somewhat worried about what she was about to hear. Art started out by telling her that Bill understood every word that they were saying. She looked over at the little dog and he was raising his head up and down for some reason.

"Ask him a yes or no question and watch his response," Art added.

After several yes or no questions, Sue Ann replied, "Alright, somehow he knows when to shake his head yes or no; but that still doesn't mean that he actually understands what we are saying."

"Ask him to go get something for you that a dog wouldn't normally get for a person," he commented.

She thought for a moment and then said, "Bill, go get Teddy's toothbrush."

While he was gone, Art told her that she could talk to him like normal and didn't need to get his attention by saying his name each time. Sure enough, in just a few moments, Bill was back with Teddy's toothbrush.

Sue Ann reached down and took the toothbrush. She was stunned and speechless; after all what was she going to say at this point.

With a big grin, Art spoke-up once more, "It even gets better. Tell him how much change you want him to bring you from the tray on our dresser."

"He can count money also," she replied?

"Go ahead, try him out," Art added.

Sue Ann was going to prove that Art was wrong; so she looked at Bill and said, "one dollar exactly in dimes."

In a matter of a few minutes Bill returned with a tissue which contained something. He gently put his front feet up on the chair where Sue Ann was sitting and laid the tissue and its contents in her lap. Sue Ann opened the tissue and to her amazement there lay ten dimes side by side.

Looking over at Art, she said, "This is amazing, what else can he do?"

"I thought you would never ask," Art replied. "What I'm going to tell you now is absolutely going to cause you to doubt my sanity, but it's true. I can actually hear what Bill thinks."

"No, I'm just not going to believe that and there's no way that you can convince me," she exclaimed!

Art said, "Alright, I'll prove it. Get one of the books from the shelf over there and show Bill a sentence in that book."

"He can read also," she inquired in amazement?

"Just do what I ask and you will see," he remarked.

Sue Ann picked up the old bible from the counter and turned it to Acts. She held the book down to where Bill could see the first verse and Art started quoting it word for word from across the room. She quickly flipped over to Psalms and once more Art started quoting the Psalm from across the room.

She looked down at Bill and said, "You can understand what I am saying?"

With this Bill shook his head up and down.

Art spoke up, "He even told me what you said to Don the other day on the phone."

Now everything was very quiet and Sue Ann knew that she would have to be a lot more careful around Bill in the future. One thing about it, if Art was crazy, then so was she.

Art went over to Sue Ann and said, "There's one final thing, but you will need to sit back down for this one."

She almost didn't want him to tell her, as this had already been a lot to learn in one day; especially concerning a dog that had been living with them for some time now.

"Remember how I sort of came back to life when the dog came along? How I took him to work with me and even changed his name?"

"Yes, but I didn't quite know what to make of it," she remarked.

"Well hold on to what sanity you still may have left," he replied. "The reason I changed his name to Bill was because JW's first name was William."

"I sort of figured that one out for myself," she smugly replied.

"Good, then you won't have any problem believing that Bill is actually JW, who has now returned in the form of this dog?"

"No, I'm definitely not buying that one," she replied.

Art looked right at her and said, "Remember that time behind the barbeque when you and Arnold kissed. You glanced over and knew that JW had walked around and caught you, didn't you?"

"It meant nothing," she said, "he and I were both feeling no pain and it just happened. Arnold wanted to make more of it but I told him no."

Looking down she asked, "Is that you JW?"

Bill just moved his head up and down once again, with what actually looked to be a smile.

"I sure wouldn't have been holding you on my lap, if I had only known that you were JW; it just wouldn't be right," she remarked.

There she had jumped on Art for talking with the dog and now she was actually talking to this same dog herself.

Smiling, Art commented, "You can't hear what he's thinking, but you can talk with him and illicit a yes or no answer. If you should want an actual answer, then you will have to ask me."

Sue Ann started asking Bill questions and Art relayed exactly what his comments were. By the time that Gina had arrived home, Sue Ann had held a very lengthy conversation with JW. This was also the most she had heard out of her husband in a really long time. Now she and Art both had a secret and neither one wanted to be caught speaking with the dog.

Gina had been diligently working at her new job for almost two months now and everyone just loved her. Lisa and Gina had shared several lunches while working together these past two months. Lisa asked several times when Gina was going to give in and at least talk with Don. Gina was stubborn and wouldn't hear of giving an inch. Lisa told her friend that he was a very eligible bachelor and even she had entertained thoughts of dating him. She hoped that this would get her friend off dead center and at least cause her to start thinking about getting back with Don. However it didn't work, as Gina simply told Lisa that she was free to date anyone she wished and Don was definitely not off limits. It was at this point when Lisa lined-up one more lunch for the two of them. When Gina walked into the restaurant that day; Don was sitting there next to Lisa.

Gina's heart simply dropped; as Lisa was a fairly beautiful woman and any man would be proud to be with her.

As Gina slid into the booth, Lisa said, "Can you believe that, they need me back at the office."

Gina might have been slow on the up-take, but she was now reading her friend perfectly. She said in a real low tone, "Thank you," as Lisa smiled and walked away.

The two of them shared a rather interesting lunch and Gina soon learned that everything Don had done was with Art's betterment in mind. She quickly forgave him for everything; even though there was really nothing to forgive him for. Both of them sat there touching, holding onto each other, and not wanting lunch to be over.

Don commented, "There was only one fatal flaw in my calculations. Art might have been talking a good game when it came to retirement, but in his heart he knew he could never bear the thought of parting from law enforcement. Being the one to unravel that next case is in his blood and he just can't help how he truly is." Don knew that this was in no small part due to Art teaming back up with JW, but he sure didn't want to cross that bridge with Gina at this time.

Gina asked, "Then what can we do before it's too late?"

"I've already put a plan into action. Let's just hope that everything and everyone is onboard for this next move, it's a duzy," he remarked.

Gina came home after a short stop over at Don's apartment and Bill instantly knew that they were once more back together. He didn't however pass this on to his old buddy Art; as he thought that the timing was just not right.

A few days later Art received another caller and this time he didn't know who the man was until he was introduced. Terr Bonnee' was the Mayor of Bayoubay, Mississippi and he was in real need of a good Police Chief. He started in explaining that the Police Department there had four officers and a horrid crime rate. He explained that none of the officers presently had the experience necessary to work investigations and these had just been piling up in the departments backlog. Terr was actually pleading with Art to come there and be their Police Chief, and of course investigator. He explained that the job didn't pay the best, but he guaranteed that there would be plenty of free benefits. Art was already drawing a retirement, so with any additional salary he should be in fairly good shape.

Art went straight to the heart of the matter and asked, "How many murders have you had in the last ten years?"

The Mayor sort of choked on that question and then said, "None, that is until two years ago and then we had two almost back to back. In Bayoubay we had always followed the process of advancing the next officer in line, each time the Chief's position came open; and this plan had served us well for many years. We had enjoyed a much laid back sleepy community and were mainly faced with fairly minor crimes; that is up until the murders. The Chief at that time tried his best to solve the two murders with no success at all. I want to warn you up front, that our somewhat preppy newspaper really laid into the old Chief and is the main reason that he left us. He had been the Chief there for almost eight years and had been with the department for going on twenty-two years. He owned a home there and had even raised his family there. I'm telling you this as it was a sad day when he finally threw his badge down on my desk. Since then the newspaper has been on my case constantly and I have not found anyone with the abilities needed; that is until I stumbled upon you."

"Yes and just exactly how did you stumble upon me," Art inquired?

The Mayor perked right up, "Why it was through your old Captain. I had been inquiring around for months now and out of the blue he called me one night at my home. We talked at length and he assured me that you were the best that he had ever seen at solving major crimes."

Art just could not believe that out of the blue his old Captain gave him any thought at all. In fact, neither he nor any of the others had even called once to check on his well being. He knew that he had a secret benefactor out there and was pretty well for sure just who it was. If this man just hadn't gone behind his back to cover-up a crime, which had now apparently worked itself out, things would have been a whole lot different. All this time Bill had been throwing his thoughts in and he was definitely ready to take on this new adventure; as life around the house there had got rather stale.

Art talked with the Mayor for the better part of two hours and told him that he needed to talk this over with Sue Ann first; prior to making any decisions. By this time Sue Ann was just returning from shopping and she at least got to meet the Mayor prior to his departure. Art explained everything to her and just waited; as he figured that she would possibly throw a fit about him even thinking about going back into law enforcement.

Sue Ann came over to him, leaned down and gave him a kiss on the cheek. She said, "If that will make you happy, then I'm all for it. I know that you and Bill are just dying to do this, so why don't we at least go down there and check this place out."

One quick phone call to the Mayor and everything was set in motion for a very grand reception and tour of the entire area. When the three of them arrived down at Bayoubay, they learned fairly quickly where it got its name from. The entire town was built on what looked to be about a mile wide bay off of a major bayou. The town was very old and quaint; as it had been kept up nicely by people who actually cared how their town looked. Sue Ann felt that the town could have actually been called Live Oak, as she had never seen so many giant trees in one place before. It was simply gorgeous how the huge trees shaded the city streets and she immediately fell in love with this picturesque little town. There were no large stores there in Bayoubay; but rather several streets full of tiny shops and overly friendly people. However, only twenty-three miles on down the road lay a town loaded with huge stores; where Sue Ann could go and shop to her heart's content. It was easy to see just how that a person could live in this beautiful community for the rest of their lives and love every minute. Art was introduced to the other officers and they all seemed excited to see that he was considering the Chief's position. He worried that the officer next in line would resent them bringing someone in from the outside; but that officer was actually more than pleased. This man had been with the department for over fifteen years and felt way more secure in his present position, than where he would be as the Cities Chief. In their tour around the city, the Mayor stopped at a few of the big beautiful homes and Art was introduced to some of the leading citizens. Most had a message for him and that was for him to not pay much attention to what the local news paper had to say about anyone or anything. After meeting several individuals that day; the Mayor purposely took Art to the newspaper office and introduced him to the lady who edited, published and owned the newspaper. She had many questions for Art and took several pictures of him, Sue Ann and even Bill. The lady promised him that she would cut him no slack; but would be fair in at least giving him a chance before passing judgment on him in her paper.

Next came Sue Ann's main interest and that was the potential homes for sale.

The Mayor seemed overly pleased to hear that they owned their own home, wanted to sell it and were interested in investing in one there locally. Property down there was higher than up north; as everything went up the closer to the coast a person came. Once the Mayor found out just what price range that they were interested in looking at, he changed hats and put on his realtor hat. For his first stop, he took them to the south city limits and then back towards the bayou. The road was only about a mile long and ended up after one turn at an absolute mansion. The front porch was to die for and the grounds were totally covered in live oaks. It was immediately evident that the place didn't have anyone carrying for it at this time and would require some work to return it to its previous state of grandeur.

Terr got out and pulled the key from his pocket. He opened the front door and they discovered that entire place was furnished; but there were sheets over everything.

He spoke-up, "When the owner died, his only child put it up for sale as is and they've had no takers."

Sue Ann started pulling the sheets off a few things and found several very valuable antiques. They went through the entire house and she was very impressed; but not nearly as much as when they stepped out onto the huge screened-in back porch. This porch was forty feet long and eighteen feet wide, with a very comfortable assortment of patio furniture. Sue Ann sat down in one of the two swings and couldn't believe what she was seeing. The view from the porch left one absolutely breathless; as it looked out over the bay with its many huge Cyprus trees. The sun was on its way down and the picturesque evening view was simply gorgeous. The loons were calling from out on the bay and the evening music was just getting started. Up until now Terr had not even mentioned the price and had only evaded the question when it was asked. Art now emphatically asked him just how much this mansion was and Terr tried once more to get out of answering. Finally he broke down and told them how much the owner was asking and it was way more than they could even think of affording. Art told him that he hoped that he was a better Mayor than realtor; as this was a total waste of their time.

It was getting late, so they put off looking at any further houses until morning. Terr then took them by the only other two possible places that they might afford and they were terribly disappointed with both of these. He had in effect ruined them by showing them the best first and now everything else just fell way short. When they left out of Bayoubay; it was with an agreement for Art and Bill to start their new job in one week, a nice apartment and an increased desire for the finer things in life. They talked all the way home about affording the mansion and each time they just came back to the fact that they just flat could not afford it. With everything that Sue Ann could come up with to convince Art, one thing just kept coming back to kill the deal for her. If they put everything they could possibly scrape together into buying this place, she wouldn't have any money left over to do anything with the place.

At one point Art asked Bill what he thought about all this and he heard, "I wish we could start tomorrow." Bill carefully kept from thinking about the house situation; as he was already keenly aware that something was playing itself out. He just wanted to watch and would hopefully enjoy the outcome.

Chapter Twelve

When Art and Sue Ann arrived home; they were surprised to see Don's SUV parked in their driveway. Sue Ann looked over at Art and said, "Now Art, please give the boy a chance."

Art was quiet and really didn't know what to think about this situation. He had thought plenty about it in the past and now fully realized that besides everything else, Don had actually taken fairly good care of his old partner. Art couldn't wait though to point out to Don that he should have played it by the book and they could have arrested the Senator. Oh well, enough with that; this new endeavor was so fascinating that he really didn't care what had happened in that whole matter before. Art made his mind up to try and reconnect his friendship with Don; partially so that he could hear the true story of how Mayor Bonnee' had actually came across his name. When they walked in the front door; they were immediately met by Gina, Teddy and Don. Gina shoved out her left hand and there was little doubt that the two of them were now married.

Sue Ann really made over the huge diamond, next to the wedding band, on Gina's hand. Then looking up at Don she said, "This is no way to start a marriage, spoiling the bride like this."

Art thrust out his hand towards Don; as he was very pleased to see the two of them back together. There was absolutely no doubt that Gina had been her happiest that year when Don stayed at their home. Don on the other hand was worried about how Art would take to all of this and was reasonably hesitant about sticking his hand out first.

When he saw Art's hand coming his direction, a huge burden was suddenly lifted from his heart, and he was pleased to see Art's acceptance in his smile. This was sure going to set the stage for everything else that he had to talk with them about and made things a whole lot easier. Art and Sue Ann had not even talked with Gina about Bayoubay; as they didn't want to say anything until it was somewhat of a reality. Now with the Don and Gina married, it meant that they could now sell the house without worrying about where Gina and Teddy would be living. This was just one more obstacle that had fallen into place and it truly looked like everything was going to work out for the best.

Don asked, "Well, what are your thoughts on Bayoubay?"

Art fairly well knew that Don had his hand in this matter and was not in the least caught off guard by this question. He remarked, "What are you talking about?"

"We don't have to play games anymore, I hope," Don replied. "Besides, I've already visited with Mayor Bonnee'."

"Then you pretty well know how everything went and what all happened," Art replied.

"Well then, tell us all about it, were dying to hear it from you," Gina added.

They went into the living room and Sue Ann started right in with what all they had seen and done. Art only managed to get a few words in and still it was easy to see that the two of them were quite taken with the little town of Bayoubay. They talked about the housing situation and even the fact that they had rented an apartment until their house was sold.

Sue Ann added, "The Mayor pretty well ruined us on the available housing though; as he showed us a beautiful mansion, which there is no hope of us ever affording.

Gina said, "Hold on to that thought for a moment; Don has something that he really needs to talk with both of you about."

Don just looked over at the two of them and said, "You don't have to do this, but at least hear me out on what I have to say." Art, Sue Ann, and Bill were all ears at this point. Bill knew that this moment would come, but he just didn't think that it would be this soon. Continuing on, Don said, "The place in Bayoubay that you call a mansion is actually the home that I was raised in and I love it there. However, my ambitions have led me away from there and I just didn't know what I was going to do with the place. I put it up for sale, but set a price so high that surely no one would ever want it. Then this whole situation came along and I just started putting a plan together. First, I would need Art retired and for him to take the job as the Police Chief of Bayoubay. Yes Art, I knew that you could not stay away from law enforcement and that was the beauty of this whole plan. Next, I could then marry the woman that I cannot live without and try to be a wonderful father to Teddy. Then finally, I must tell you that I have political ambitions in this district; so I would need to own a home and live here. Being that both Gina and I are only children, this could actually work out perfectly. Both of my parents have passed away and the house belongs totally to me. What I propose is for us to trade homes and then the two of you can leave us the so called mansion when you're through with it. Both Art and Sue Ann were speechless, but Bill was absolutely going crazy. He could definitely see himself taking leisurely strolls among the many live oaks on that place.

Then he broke it to Art that he smelled Don in that house from the very first moment, but just didn't let on. Art didn't even act like he had heard this and Bill wondered if he truly had heard him; so he stayed after him for a comment.

Art simply looked down at Bill and said, "Later my friend."

Sue Ann and Don were both aware of what was happening and just smiled at Art.

Once more it was Sue Ann that took the lead as she said, "You mean that you would just trade houses with us?"

"That's right," Don remarked.

"But what if something happens to where that you can't get it back," she asked?

"That's just something that I've decided not to worry about," he replied.

Sue Ann looked over at Art and then said, while absolutely jumping for joy, "Then yes, we'll trade."

Art spoke-up, "Not so fast, my new son-in-law and I need to discuss this over a few beers."

Sue Ann remarked, "Discuss all you want, but we're moving to the mansion."

The men proceeded outside and it was a fairly nice fall evening. Don was hoping that the last case they worked on would not come up; but sure enough Art asked him if he would mind sharing just what all went on there. Actually Art was feeling pretty good about this situation now, with the Senators confession and all.

Don started in, "Art, I need to tell you a story to start with and I hope you find it interesting enough to possibly look into."

Art was all ears as he leaned back and took a long draw off of his beer. Don continued, "While I was in the process of finishing up my schooling; I learned that my father had a very serious heart problem. Every chance I got, I went home to check on him; but he lived there alone and wouldn't hear of anyone moving in to care for him. In his shirt pocket he always carried a bottle of nitro pills; with one loose pill just so he wouldn't have to worry about taking the lid off in an emergency. Everyone in town knew what shape he was in and knew that he could go at any moment. Nitro pills can save your life, but they can also kill if you have a heart condition and take too many. The Mayor told you that they had two murders within only a few days. I personally believe that it was actually three. You see, they found my father sitting out on the patio at about that same time and they ruled his death as being from natural causes. With the two other murders to worry about, I believe they rushed to proclaim my father's death due to natural causes. The coroner ruled that he had nitro in his system and that he had taken the nitro to stop the affects of a heart attack without success. I have very serious doubts about that due to the free pill in his pocket still being there. If he had felt a heart attack coming on, then he would have taken that pill first. Somehow I just know that his death was tied to the other two murders."

"That does sound suspicious," Art commented. "I'll have to keep this in the back of my mind, as I'm working this case. But how does that figure in with our last case?"

"Well from the very first case that we worked together, I admired your abilities and wished that it was you that was working on the murders in Bayoubay. Then when I learned about yours and Bills joint abilities; I knew that I wanted you to look into my father's death. We had worked together for some time when the Chief quite his job down there and I want you to know that I had nothing to do with that. However, it was only with the high profile case involving the Senator that my plan was finally formed and put it into motion. I hated not being able to tell you, Gina or anyone about it; but I had my reasons. You see if everything had backfired on me; I sure didn't want any of you to be drug down with me. Everything was really falling into place though and was going very well when the Senator killed himself. That was definitely not in my planning and was due to unforeseen circumstances."

Art asked, "What circumstances, like he was covering up for his son?"

"Well he thought he was, but in truth he had been tricked into believing that his son had actually killed Troyla." Art was all ears as Don continued. "What happened after the Senator's death actually unraveled everything. I already knew that Tremain had been the one that killed the girl; but I needed proof though that he had also caused the Senator's death. Remember the red wine that was all over the floor and walls?"

He definitely had Arts attention and Art acknowledged his memory of the red wine mess.

Don went on, "It was that wine that finally sealed the deal. I had no time frame for the wine being on the floor and only one set of foot prints in the wine. If it had been there the entire time then there would have been three sets of footprints in the wine. It was evident that someone, most likely Troyla, had thrown the wine glass and wine; as it trailed off of the bed. However, Tremain's footprints were the only tracks in the spilt wine; so he must have been the last person leaving that room."

Art asked, "But didn't you send off her fingernail scrapings and didn't they come back as a match for the Senator?"

"You know, it must have slipped my mind, and I just know that those scrapings must be among the evidence somewhere."

"How much did the Senator pay you to loose those scrapings," Art inquired?

"Absolutely nothing, but he did perform a few favors; which helped several individuals. One in fact was you; whether you knew it or not at the time."

Art replied, "It took me some time to come around to that fact, but I finally did."

"Yes and this played directly into my plans of getting you down to Bayoubay. I knew from the very first that you were not the kind of person that could simply retire and would be interested in something like they would be offering."

"Before we go there, lets finish what we were discussing about the Senator. Didn't his son kill the girl," Art asked?

"No, but he lawyered-up from the very first, because he felt that his father had killed her. When his father killed himself and left the suicide note confessing; the son just knew that he was right." Art wasn't even breaking in at this time and was all ears. "I helped the officers work the Senators suicide and there on his desk was a small melted pile of plastic, from something that he had deliberately burned. We sent it off to be analyzed; but before it even came back I discovered what it was. You see the Senator's son came to see me and handed me a tiny digital recorder. I played the recording and knew exactly what had happened. Speaking with the Senator's son; I learned that he knew Troyla had another boyfriend. Hiring a private detective; he learned that she had been seeing this boyfriend at that hotel on a regular basis. It was the Senator's son who had actually taken his father's 38 from the house, to go scare the boyfriend off.

However, when he arrived at the hotel door, it was open and his father's voice was what he heard coming from the room. Daniel didn't know what to think so he hid. When his father left, he went back to the room. He had the 38 in his hand and the girl screamed. He saw that it was scaring her so he laid it down. Looking at her naked there on that bed, he was repulsed and told her that they were through. She got mad, told him that he would be back and he knew it. Daniel told me that as he turned to leave, she threw the glass of wine at him, but it missed and hit the wall. He said that he never returned after that and last saw the pistol just lying there in the room. But upon listening to the small recorder; shortly after this the girl was heard to say no and two shots were heard. What came with that recorder was the clincher. It was a letter explaining that the individual had presented his request to the father; when he should have went straight to the son from the first. It required that five million dollars be paid or the person would take the recording straight to the authorities. With this and the shoeprint evidence, I was able to acquire a warrant for Tremain's apartment. There we found the mother lode. The original recording that had been altered to implicate the son and the 38 that had been used in the killing. Just this morning Tremain pled guilty to take the death penalty off his plate. He told the whole story as part of the deal. He felt that Troyla had now lost her chance at making millions off of the Senator; but saw a whole different possibility in setting the son up for her murder."

Art was speechless for a few moments and then finally said, "I'm just glad that this whole matter is over and we're back together."

Don put his head down and said, "Art, this case has made me take a hard look at myself and I'm not for sure that I like what I see. My father raised me to go into politics and has practically choreographed my entire life. I've very much become an opportunist and have already made the moves necessary to secure myself a seat in the Mississippi Senate. But what is my life really worth anyway?"

This was the furthest thing from what Art could imagine and he definitely wanted to say something at this time that would help and possibly even make at least a little sense. He spoke-up, "You've already helped a lot of people in your life and that's something that most cannot say after a life time. A seat on the Senate would just give you the ability to help even more. I feel that your father was a wise man; because now you will be able help our brothers in law enforcement, even more than anyone else."

They were both quiet now and just sat back and enjoyed another beer. Life was good and only getting better at this point. Inside the house Sue Ann was still in unbelief and wanted Gina to go and look at the house that they were trading them. Even before the men were sober enough to make any decisions, the women had decided that there would be a return trip this next weekend to Bayoubay. Neither Sue Ann nor Gina knew of Don's suspicions; concerning his father being murdered in that very house.

Chapter Thirteen

That was a very busy week for both families; as Don and Gina started moving into the master bedroom as fast as Art and Sue Ann were packing to move out. They all agreed that the furniture would stay with the houses and as such nothing large really needed to be moved. Art's new job required him to purchase a vehicle to be used on the job and he was to be reimbursed through a standard government vehicle allowance. He had not owned a pickup in several years; but felt that a new pickup would possibly be the best option in an area such as that. When this whole group left out on Friday evening, it looked like a regular caravan; with Art's new pickup, Sue Ann's car and Don's SUV packed full with all of their possessions. Sue Ann absolutely couldn't wait to get back and look at the place that was now going to be theirs. Gina had already been told so much about this place that she felt as if she had already been there. When they arrived the sun was just setting and the view across the bay was once more absolutely breathtaking. Don went in and turned the lights on for them and then Bill noticed a vehicle sitting down near the boat house. Don, Art and Bill started down that direction, with Bill running well ahead of them. When Bill got close enough, Art heard that the vehicle was that of one of the City Police Officers. In specific it was Officer Ronnie Fallon, known to all as Ron around the area. Ron had been on the Police Department for going on twelve years now and had grown up there near Bayoubay. This place was out of the city limits, so Art wondered just why that Ron would be down there.

Ron came out of his police vehicle when he recognized Don and Art. He was alone and came to meet them. He said, "I wondered who was messing around up there at the old house; hasn't been anyone around there for almost two years now."

Art spoke-up, "I'm buying it from Don and will be moving in here real soon."

"Well I'll get out of your way then. I just love to come out here in the evenings to watch the sun go down across the bay," Ron remarked.

Once Ron was gone, Art noticed the amount of traffic that had been to this location and pointing it out to Don. Art commented, "I don't have a good feeling about this. Something strange has been going on here."

Don replied, "Then for goodness sake, don't trust him. I don't trust anyone in this town besides the Mayor; but then I have a bias."

Bill made some rounds down in that area and reported back to Art. For the best of his abilities, Ron had been here many times and was always alone. While walking back up to the house, Bill took off and then reported back to Art that he didn't pick up on any fresh scents around the outside of the house. Entering the house the men found that the women were already busy pulling the cloths of the furniture and were in full evaluation mode. Sue Ann came to the conclusion that they would need all new appliances and possibly even a total kitchen make-over. Art just smiled and knew that Sue Ann was at home in her new surroundings. The remainder of the weekend was filled with cleaning, unloading and planning.

Don, Gina and Teddy roamed the grounds and Don showed her every one of his childhood places, where he went to escape. Many times in the huge live oaks, he dreamed that he was a pirate on a massive ship and they were just preparing to board an innocent merchant ship. Several of the ropes still hung down from where he swung aboard the make-believe ship or tree next to the one he was in. He was practically as nimble as a squirrel and could scamper quickly through the various trees. Needless to say, Gina was very impressed and could just see Teddy following in Don's footsteps; as they came regularly to see her parents.

Monday morning Art was ready for his first day at work and Sue Ann was going to visit with the Mayor about possible local contractors. Art and Sue Ann had rented an apartment on their previous trip to Bayoubay. However, the Mayor had already taken care of this situation, as he had been working with Don all along. Upon showing up at the rather small shotgun style police station, Art was met by all four officers and Mayor Bonnee'. Everyone was interested in just what changes he might make and what new policies he might implement. The Mayor wanted to have the first say on any changes and wanted Art's ear before he stepped off and did something that he might regret. The officers all stood outside and visited, while Art and the Mayor spent over two hours in Arts new office. The Mayor was concerned that Art might get off on the wrong foot and alienate the citizens there in Bayoubay early on. He told Art that he and the citizens were very concerned with the fact that the killer or killers had not been brought to justice; but he was way more concerned with just how Art would handle future crimes. He assured Art that the old Chief had lost everyone's faith in his abilities way before the murders came along. His suggestion was that Art constantly consider the murders, but spend most of his time in solving the many petty crimes that presently plagued their City. Art agreed that cases closed were paramount to a successful department. When he came out of his meeting with the Mayor; he addressed the officers and learned that all of them had at least ten years with the department. Up until this time longevity meant everything, including advancement. However, Art's mere presence meant the end to longevity as they knew it. He spoke with the officers in a very non restrictive manor and emphasized the need for them to work together in collecting good evidence.

When he thought he was through, one of the men asked, "What's your policy on tickets?"

Art asked, "Just what should my policy be?" This started a mountain of comments and Art finally ended it with, "It's very evident that all four of you hold different opinions on this matter; even though you have been here a lot longer than I have. My policy at least at this time is for you to follow what you feel and bring no grief upon me. If we start having problems, then we will reconsider this policy. The men then wanted to know what their shifts would be and were fairly worried about what changes he might implement. Art surprised them all by telling them that he wanted them to work out their shifts between themselves and get back with him. They immediately took off trying to figure out just what would be best for each of them. Salaries were not the best on this department and most of these men had second jobs. All of this had to be taken into accord and not much really changed when the men finally brought the schedule back to Art.

He commented, "I will require you to remain within this jurisdiction while you're on duty, unless circumstances come up to where you have to leave." He knew that this would put a burden on Ron, as he had evidently been going out to the Claybourn estate daily, for some time now. He watched Ron as he said this and his head was hung low.

What Art didn't realize was that Ron had asked Mr. Claybourn if he could fish from his dock and had been for a good amount of time prior the old man's death.

However, when Bill checked around he didn't smell Ron's odor on the dock and really didn't think much of it at the time. With everything in fair order, Art took off to survey his new realm. He had been a reactive police officer in his carrier up to this point and now he was going to have to be proactive. He stopped at several locations where people were gathered, introduced himself and asked what they expected of him. Most were really surprised that the new Police Chief even cared what they thought. Art wrote down names, phone numbers, and asked them if they minded him calling them. The thing he heard the most was that they were tired of the constant crime, but definitely wanted him to be fair with all. This was almost a contradiction of feelings and left Art with the opinion that most of them at least had a fair idea of just who was involved.

His first case came the following morning; when a person called and reported that someone had removed the GPS locater from his car during the night. Art was the one who took the call; as no other officers came to work before noon on the weekdays. He and Bill showed up at the location of the theft and Bill immediately went to work. The individual reporting the missing GPS locater had failed to report that he had also lost a pistol. Bill smelled the gun powder and quickly alerted Art. Art asked the man if he was missing anything else and he sort of stammered around a little, indicating that he knew the pistol was missing.

Art asked, "What caliber of pistol was it?"

The man was totally shocked to hear that this officer was already aware that a gun was missing. He told Art all about it and the fact that it was a fully loaded 9mm. A shiver went up Art's back just thinking of who might have this ticking time bomb. Bill on the other hand had not been sitting still and already had a trail for them to follow. He informed Art of just what he was doing and took off down the street. About two houses down Bill went up into a driveway and approached a car parked there. At this point nothing had been reported as being stolen from this car. Going up to the door, Art introduced himself and asked the woman at the door if she would see if anything was missing from her car. The young woman immediately became concerned, as she had failed to bring her purse in last night and it had six one hundred dollar bills in it. Quickly checking the car seat; she found her purse poured out and the money was now missing.

Bill let Art know that there were two of them, young males, and they had traveled there on bicycles; as he had already located their tire prints. The little town only had two overnight night convenience stores and Art fairly well knew that the young thieves would have to spend some of their ill gotten gains, before the night was over. He went to both of the convenience stores and at one Bill told him that he had picked up on the young men's scents. Speaking with the clerk on duty, he was not the one who had worked all night; but at least was able to give Art the other clerks address. Art went by that address and after thoroughly pounding on the door; he finally got the man up and out of bed.

While Art was speaking with him, Bill informed him that the gun in question was in this very apartment and the odor was on this man. Instantly Art pulled his pistol and put the muzzle against the clerks face.

He asked, "Who else is here?"

The thoroughly terrified clerk responded, "No one except for me."

Art told him that he knew the stolen 9mm was in this apartment and would get a warrant if the man didn't come clean. The clerk told him that he didn't know that it was stolen and had only bought it last night from two young boys. Finally he admitted trading them beer and cigarettes for the pistol. He didn't know the boys names, but knew that they had been in there late at night on several occasions. Bill picked up on the boys trail from the back of the store and it was a lot fresher than before. He followed it only about two blocks before he indicated which house they had entered. There laying in the yard were the two bicycles. Art went up to the house and informed the man and woman that came to the door, that he was investigating several burglaries from last night and on previous nights. He could read in the father's face that he was not in the least surprised and the mother was definitely ready to cover up for anything the boys may have done.

Art went straight to the heart of the situation and told them that the boys had stolen a gun last night. This changed both parent's demeanor drastically and they immediately wanted him to search the boy's room. The boys were both still passed out at this time, as they had stayed up all night stealing whatever they could find. Drinking a beer behind the convenience store had definitely done them in and they simply cratered when they made it home. From what Art found in that room, the boys had been out on many nights and had been a good part of what the city feared. They were both eleven years old and were

children of previous marriages. He was well aware
that the boys wouldn't get much from the justice
system, so he cut them a deal. He told them that if they
would work with him to get everyone's things back, he
wouldn't press charges but would only put them on
probation. He also told them that if they did
everything they were supposed to, this whole matter
would be erased from their permanent record. Art
realized that the juvenile offenses were never
maintained on permanent records; so he really wasn't
lying to the boys. The young men, as he chose to refer
to them, did their best to get everything back to the
rightful owners. This entire situation opened up
several doors; as the young men told who had
purchased their stolen goods, with the full knowledge
that they were truly stolen. Art was already gaining a
considerable reputation around this small town. In
fact, more people were now coming to him and telling
him just what they knew about what had been going
on around there. This led to the investigation into an
organized fencing ring and a fact that he didn't want to
hear.   At one point he had to call one of his officers in
and it wasn't going to be good. He learned that this
officer was actually buying stolen guns and as such
was personally facilitating the thieves. When he called
the officer in, he allowed him to resign and turn States
evidence against the fencing ring. In return the man
was allowed to leave town with no legal charges
pending against him. With this situation under his
belt, Art was now somewhat of a local hero. In every
case someone had suffered a loss; but at this same time
this was a small tight-knit community. Each and every
criminal was related to several others that lived there
and cared somewhat for him or her. Art's compassion
was what everyone was talking about and they were
proud to have him as their Police Chief. He had now

proved that he would even clean-up the corruption within his own department.

In the process of daily visiting with the citizens; he learned that one of their greatest concerns was with the dogs that were released to run loose at night. They had a city dog catcher, but he went in at four each evening and by five o'clock dogs were being let out everywhere to run the streets. There were several reasons for this situation and laziness was at the top of the list. People just didn't want to take on the responsibility of getting their dogs exercise; so they just let them out to do as they pleased during the evening and night hours. This situation had actually brought neighbor against neighbor; as dogs always seemed to go out of their own yards to do their business. Neighbors had BB guns at ready to keep stray dogs out of their yards. However, this was not the real problem; but rather the drugies and thieves that would let their Pit bulls, Rottweilers, and Dobermans just run free after dark. There were certain streets that no one dared walk down at night. Art knew that he had to take these streets back to make the citizens feel more at ease. This was a wonderful little town and just didn't need a problem such as this. Several times the City Council had been contacted with this problem and each time they came up with no lasting solutions. Art on the other hand didn't even ask for permission, but rather went out on foot patrol at night with Bill. What Art thought was that no dog running free could resist the urge to confront the small spotted dog that had somehow recklessly ventured into their territory. When in fact, it was Art who drew more attention from the more vicious dogs than Bill. In each and every case Art would let them get in close and then he would administer a healthy dose of pepper spray.

Pepper spray was better than a base ball bat and would stop a vicious dog in just about the same amount of time. However, it would take weeks for the affects to wear off; as the dogs didn't know to wash it off. One good dose of pepper spray and that particular dog would not run out to confront anyone, ever again. Vicious dogs were instantly ruined as far as their owners were concerned. After about two weeks of their walking the streets at night, the dog complaints fell off drastically. Art wasn't made the hero in the local paper; as he preferred that this situation go unrecognized. However, he had run into a few concerned citizens at night and they all seemed to be fairly well pleased. One in fact, at about midnight this one night, called out to Art so he came over to visit with this citizen. The citizen suggested that Art not go out in the white shirts anymore at night; as it left him a very identifiable target. This sounded like very sensible advice, so Art bought several dark colored shirts for duty at night. Then on another night, an older woman invited him in for some fresh peach cream cobbler and homemade peach ice-cream. Art felt that it was only neighborly to take her up on this offer and all the way home Bill reminded him that peach cream cobbler was his absolute favorite.

When Art went to replace the officer that he had to let go, he was sorely disappointed with the ones that had applied. However, he couldn't blame them with the salary being offered there for a beginning officer. The City was definitely wrong in setting their beginning wage so low. It didn't matter if the officer applying had six months experience or ten years; the City only paid a certain amount for a beginning wage. How in the world could they expect to have a Police Department worth anything with practices such as these? Art was somewhat pleased with the resume' of one of the female applicants; as he felt that she could really make a good addition to the Department. He was right about her; Karen showed up at every location where an officer was sent and did her best to help everyone. After considerable discussion with the Mayor; Art acquired funding to send her off to crime scene investigation school. He promised the Mayor that with her help he would be able to close even more cases.

Chapter Fourteen

      Having a grand home with such massive grounds was really going to require a lot of upkeep and Art noticed that Mr. Claybourn didn't seem to own a lawnmower. It would have just come natural for a person of his age and were-for-all to have hired out his lawn work. In making his rounds across the city, Art ran into several individuals that asked if he had anything for them to do. However, not one individual mentioned that he had previously taken care of the Claybourn grounds. Art was extremely hesitant in hiring just anyone and besides he had just bought one of those rather expensive zero turn mowers. Watching how the young men there in town abused and rough-housed on their own mowers, simply caused him to be doubly leery of hiring anyone young. Besides, Art was having a blast mowing his own property with this wonderful new machine. He definitely had a new toy and was getting to learn the lay of his domain. This place was comprised of about ten acres, but the brush and vines had only been kept at bay over an area approximately four hundred feet wide and seven hundred feet in deep. The end of the property ran all the way down a low winding hill to the bay in the back. Art was simply amazed with the flying squirrels and would shut the mower down and watch as they seemed to migrate from tree to tree as he moved their direction. Bill on the other hand couldn't keep from chasing them, even if he knew that he would never consider catch one. This love of mowing and nature shortly grew old though; as it seemed as if the grass grew even faster than Art could keep up with it. With his requirement that the officers stay within their jurisdiction while on duty, he felt it only right that he followed these same rules. As a result, all of his mowing fell to the evenings he was free and the weekends when he wasn't being called out. Just owning this place, Art was truly working harder and enjoying life less. Sue Ann had even tried to bring a beer out to where he was mowing; but Art had quickly learned that it took both hands to operate a zero turn mower. Not that he wouldn't stop for a good cold beer though and he sure appreciated her bringing it out to him. Bill usually found a good shady spot to watch from, as Art pulled up to take the beer from Sue Ann. On more than a few occasions, he made Art aware that he sure missed a good cold beer himself. Art would wait until the beer was almost gone and then he would call Bill for a taste. That's all it took and Bill was satisfied; as it definitely didn't taste like he remembered.

Sue Ann had also been busy in the house and everything was really starting to come together. Her not having a job allowed her to concentrate all of her energies on making everything just right. With the extra money they still had from Art's retirement bonus, she was able to totally remodel the kitchen. Now with all the stainless steel and granite in place, the kitchen was absolutely gorgeous. She felt a very satisfying degree of achievement and wanted to show it off to everyone. They had started making a few new friends and it was time for a very grand party. This was to be one of their two day parties and Sue Ann had everything that anyone could possibly want. Art made the officers aware that he was not to be bothered this weekend; unless that is if one of them just happened to be dying. Normally he was always on call, but he wanted this weekend to be special for Sue Ann's sake.

Then one day out of nowhere, Bill let Art know
that he wanted to go visit his sister. Art was not so
sure about this; but she really didn't live that far away.
He told Bill that he would be glad to take him to see his
sister. A phone call was made to Lea Belle and she told
him that she had been expecting his call. This
statement caught Art by surprise; as he had long forgot
that he had promised her he would return one day and
fill her in on everything. Well actually he hadn't said
those exact words; but he hadn't said anything to the
contrary when she asked him to come back and tell her
everything. Sue Ann already had plans for the day that
they were to go see Lea Belle and this trip shouldn't
take over a few hours anyway. When they arrived it
was early in the morning; so Lea Belle asked Art and
Bill in for some tea. Walking into the house, the very
first thing Art noticed was a rather large picture of Bill.
This had been painted from a photograph that Lea
Belle had taken the last time they visited with her. This
picture however was not an enlargement of the photo,
but rather an oil painting done by Lea Belle herself.
She had quite the eye for detail and had made Bill out
to be very majestic.

She saw that they had noticed the picture; so
she stopped and admired it with them.

No one said one word until she broke the
silence, "Art, you may not realize it, but I truly feel that
Bill here is my brother reincarnated."

Neither Art nor Bill said anything and Art
suddenly felt very uneasy. What if Bill wanted to tell
her and she wanted to keep Bill there with her. Art
kept waiting for something from Bill, but nothing was
forth coming. Bill then just walked over to his sister
and put his head up against her leg. She reached down
to scratch on him and could tell that he wanted to be
picked up.

Art commented, "I'm surprised, he usually doesn't allow anyone to pick him up."

Lea Belle came back with, "I believe that he too knows who he was in his former life."

They proceeded to the back patio and Art just had to say something, "He knows what we're saying and can actually understand."

"I knew it," she said, "He is JW."

"Ask him anything that can be answered by a yes or no answer and watch his response," Art added.

She started asking Bill questions and was utterly amazed to see his responses.

The only time that Bill refused to answer was when Lea Belle would ask him if he was JW reincarnated. This went on for almost two hours and then Lea Belle asked Bill if he knew any tricks. Bill started through the things that he could do and Lea Belle was convinced that this truly was her brother. Finally she asked if he wanted to stay there with her and Bill ran over and got on Art's lap. With Bill on his lap, Art told her how wonderful it had been working with Bill and how he always wants to go on all the police calls with him.

Lea Belle told them how much she had looked forward to this day and hoped that they would come back soon; as she just knew that she might even be able to communicate further with Bill.

Art and Bill both left out of there that day with approximately as much apprehension as on their first visit. Just as on the previous visit, neither of them could see the need to return. Not once had Lea Belle asked anything about their brother or his girlfriend.

All this time Art had not just turned a blind eye to the two previous murders; but had studied each at length. He actually felt that the old Chief had probably done as well as he possibly could, considering the circumstances. In each of these cases Art had let Bill examine the pieces of evidence. The only common thread in all of this was Ron's odor. However, it's just possible that he could have been the officer processing the evidence and that would explain just how his odor was on everything. Art knew that he needed to visit with the old Chief and found out where that he was working at this time. Visiting with him Art learned that he had really come down in the world from Bayoubay. In fact, the old Chief was now a night watchman at a fishing camp. He was very surprised to hear of the officer buying the stolen property and admitted that he had no indication of that happening. Inquiring into Ron, the old Chief told him that Ron was probably the best officer that he had. This worried Art, so he asked what made him feel that way. The old Chief relayed that during the time of the murders; Ron worked straight through for well over forty eight hours and had helped him process every piece of the evidence. When Art asked if they had processed anything for DNA; the old Chief said that several items had been sent off, but no foreign DNA was found. The Chief let Art know that the perpetrator must have worn gloves.

Worried even more about this now, Art asked, "Did you and Ron send in DNA samples, so they could be eliminated from the findings?"

"Why yes, that was our standard procedure back then," he remarked.

Art let this whole matter drop right there, as he didn't know how tight the old Chief and Ron actually were. Back at the office, Art asked one of the other officers if he had latex gloves to use at the crime scenes. He found out that for years now the EMS service had been furnishing them with boxes of these gloves. Then he asked the officer if he had ever seen any of the others picking up evidence without the gloves actually being on. The answer was no surprise, as the man said that sadly enough he had.

By this time Karen had completed her crime scene investigation training and Art was ready to speak with the Mayor once more. He took Karen with him and was fully prepared for the Mayor's objections. Sure enough when he broke it to the Mayor that he needed an additional officer and wanted to increase Karen's pay; he got what he expected.

Art broke into the Mayor's usual reply with, "I know who committed the murders, but the evidence collection was so poor that I can't prove it. Possibly we won't have another murder; even though the murderer still lives here. However, if the evidence collection does not get substantially better by that time; he will probably get off once more and it will be your fault."

The Mayor puffed up like a toad and spoke-out, "Let's see if I understand you right; you want an evidence officer in case we have another murder and this individual will be of no use to us unless there is another murder."

"Wrong my dear Watson. An evidence officer could come out and help all the other officers with their cases by collecting all the evidence; while freeing the officers up to continue with their investigations. This evidence officer would fine tune their skills by collecting evidence daily. Let's say that we have a rape tonight, this officer would be invaluable."

By this time the Mayor was rubbing his chin and that meant that he was now in thinking mode instead of rejection mode.

Art spoke-up, "We'll just leave you to think about this and you can get back with us when you get it all figured out."

They left out and Karen asked, "Does this mean that I get a raise?"

Smiling, Art answered, "Not just yet, but it wouldn't surprise me if you did."

Sure enough the Mayor got the City Council to go along with the proposal and they also collectively wanted to commend Art on what he had already accomplished in his short time in their little City. A fifth officer was hired and Art broke the news to all the officers that Karen was now the official crime scene investigation officer for the department. She was to be on call 24 hours a day and seven days a week. Her only time away from the department had to be covered by Art himself. This arrangement pleased Karen; as she just loved it there in Bayoubay and could pursue her other interests right from her home.

Art had pretty well hit a dead end with the previous murders and was going to need something new to surface before he could go much further. He picked up the phone and relayed to Don that even though he was pretty well for sure that Ron was the killer; he just couldn't get a grip on anything that might cause this whole thing to unravel. Don on the other hand had good news though; the Senate had approved of his efforts towards carrying out the remaining term of Senator Whitney. Not only this, but he had also been placed on a Major Crime Oversight Committee.

He asked Art, "Just how do you feel about extra-unusual crime investigation techniques."

Art chuckled as he said, "You sure asked the right question that time. Here I am taking directions from a small spotted dog and you want to know if I believe in the unusual. Was that supposed to be a joke or something?"

"No joke," he replied, "I've learned that there's a very eclectic group that meets to solve major crimes.

They're from all across the country and only handle one case at a time. Our only shot at them looking into this case is your talking to that spotted dog. I can try and get you a meeting with them; but what you have to realize is that everyone there is just as special in their own ways as the two of you are. For one thing they are very open about what their abilities are and negativity is instantly rejected. If I get you that appointment, then from the very first moment you need to tell them what it is that you and Bill can bring to their illustrious group. Be very open about everything and possibly they will bring you in as a member. Art, this is just about our only chance at solving my father's murder."

"You make this sound extra-unusual," Art commented.

Don pled with him, "Art please take this serious, if for no other reason than for my sake. Remember, if I get you audience with them, you have to be just as believing as they are."

Art got serious and said, "You make it sound as if we were joining some sort of secret club."

"If they accept you, then you will be," Don remarked. "It's the chance of a life time and these people work for the FBI and all the larger agencies; however, no one is to know anything about their involvement. Couldn't you just see some smart aleck attorney finding out about you and Bill; then questioning you on the witness stand about where you get your information from?"

Now actually serious, Art remarked, "Don, I promise you that we will both do our best if we do get an audience with this group."

Don wasn't as sure, so he asked if he and Gina could come for the weekend to celebrate his new appointment. In addition he asked if there was any way that Sue Ann might be venturing on down to the coast; because he would sure like for her to bring back about a dozen blue crabs if she did. Boiled blue crab was definitely a local delicacy, which few enjoyed the further from the coast that you were located. The weekend that they showed up, Sue Ann put on a wonderful meal of red beans and rice, topped off with freshly boiled blue crab. Everyone ate until they could eat no more, so Don mentioned that they needed to get out and take a walk. He had already bragged on what the old place was looking like and now was very interested in walking around to see everything that Art had accomplished. Once down at the boat house, Don asked if Ron had been back since the night they found him there. Art told him that he always knew when Ron was anywhere near, as Bill would start growling. He let Don know that on a few occasions they had seen Ron pull up the driveway, turn around and then leave.

"There's got to be something out there in the bay, but what is it," Art asked?

"No telling, but whatever it is, it's already caused him to kill three people," Don remarked.

Then Art asked, "Who did your father use to mow this place anyway?"

Thinking about it for a moment, Don replied, "Tom Hewitt, one of the men found dead."

"Well that's one of the ties to your father, but it's pretty thin," Art remarked.

"How about the other man, Winston Rheims, did he ever work here for your father?"

"You do know that Winston was not his actual name, but just what everyone called him. When he was a younger man he always had a Winston behind his ear, just in case of an emergency. He was a local day laborer and I'm for sure that he probably did some work from time to time for my father."

As they were walking; Don took the opportunity to talk with Art about the unorthodox crime investigation unit that he had mentioned to him. They were referred to as, "*The Gray Area*," and rightfully so; as most of their techniques would definitely not hold up in a court of law. Art was already very aware that everything wasn't black and white; and as such there were huge amounts of daily police work that definitely fell within the gray area. However, not even this would stretch to *The Gray Area* that Don was speaking of at this time.

Don spoke-up, "They are always willing to give anyone a chance; but you will definitely have to prove your worth."

That weekend just before Don left, he looked over at Art and said, "Be at this address in Baton Rouge, Louisiana on the 12th promptly at 8:00 in the morning." With this Don held out his hand and handed Art a red key and an address, "Good luck my friend, I'm counting on you."

The mystery involved in all of this was almost chilling; but Art looked forward to meeting these people. In the days leading up to the 12th of that month, Art pretty well told all of the officers that he was going to a meeting which could possibly shed light on the local murders. He had not told any of them where he was going or who it actually was that he would be seeing there. Most of them didn't really seem interested; but Ron finally got around to asking him where he would be if they needed to get hold of him. Art told him that he couldn't tell them anything at this time, but might have something for them very shortly. This caused Ron to be suspicious that Art might actually be hiding something from him for some unknown reason.

Chapter Fifteen

Art and Bill showed up at the address in Baton Rouge on the 12th at about fifteen minutes before the time that they should have been there. Art had put on his best suite and hoped that it would be good enough for this group. The place looked like an old southern mansion, except for the business like parking lot out front; which was dotted with several various cars, trucks, and SUVs. They walked up the front steps and found that the door was locked and had no key hole. There also was no door bell, but it did have an unusually large and old fashioned door knocker. Art rang the knocker three times and the building sounded absolutely hollow inside. Bill decided that he needed to look around, so he took off around the side of the building. In just a few moments he returned and told Art that there was a red door with a key hole out back. They proceeded around the building and Art found a red door with no handle, but a key hole in the center of the door. He found that his key fit the door lock; but would not turn once inserted. Upon pulling the key out, they found that the door swung open for them. They proceeded through the open door and Bill said that he didn't smell where anyone else had entered through that door recently. When they were well inside, the door shut behind them and this time there was no key hole on this side. Proceeding down a rather short hallway that gradually narrowed; they entered the only door there and it was already open. This door led to a rather small room with only two chairs inside. One entire wall was a mirror and Art knew well what this room was used for. He had no doubt that he was about to be interrogated and he just needed to keep his cool.

Sitting down he told Bill, "Well I guess we both know what they use this room for."

Bill jumped up in the other chair and remarked, "They sure are going to every end to protect themselves. This should really be interesting."

Finally about fifteen minutes later, a voice came as if it was actually the walls speaking. It said, "Thank you for taking time out of your busy schedule to come here today." Bill kept very quiet and finally the voice continued. "Art, we understand that you and Bill have a remarkable relationship. One which allows you to have insight into crime scenes, which no other officer has. We here at *The Gray Area* are the same and as such the rest of the world treats us as if we are strange, different, or even crazy. This is why we go to such great lengths to protect our abilities and identities. Several major crime fighting organizations use us; but even they are limited as to who gets to know anyone within this unit. If we decide that you are approved, then you will become part of this unit for life. You will still be able to live a rather normal life for the most part. However, when we are called in to examine a major crime scene, then you might be called up to assist us. Once you are in you will get to meet the others; but at no time will you contact any of them for any reason. The only contact you will have with them will be on the case that we are all working on at that time. If at any time you do not think that you are interested, then you are free to leave and will find the door you entered open."

Art finally spoke-up, "We'll stay, but what do we do next?"

Our little group only works on one crime at a time to keep from contaminating any of our abilities.

We understand that Bill is supposedly your expartner reincarnated as a dog. It would also seem that you supposedly read his thoughts and that assists you at a crime scene. You would have to admit that this would stretch anyone's beliefs, but here at *The Gray Area* we are just as unbelievable. We will be releasing a few scents into the room, which you could not possibly detect, and we want you to tell us what it is that Bill smells.

In a couple of minutes Art started in, "Bananas, jalapeno peppers, paper money, cocaine, cigar smoke, sweat from a white male, fish, pistol powder, Swiss cheese, methamphetamine, hair from a black female, toothpaste, almonds, cedar, cut grass, pine needles, dead body, body fluids, marijuana, bleach, plastic, cat hair, charcoal, lemon peel, doctors office."

The voice came back, "Very nice, in fact much better than what we had hoped for. Now for some of the more difficult items. Take your time with these odors."

Once again Art reported, "Sweat from a black male, body fluids, blood, cooked eggs, sausage, toast, and coffee. Motel bedding with body fluids from multiple donors, both male and female. Live chickens, Hispanic female, chili powder, and olives. A reptile, shoe leather, polish, and a white male. Hair spray, wig hair, dandruff, cigarette smoke, and a black female. Tuna fish on rye, onion, sweet pickles, lettuce, and mayo.

Once again they stopped their tests and remarked on how amazed that they truly were. Their next test involved Bills sense of hearing and he passed everything with flying colors. At this point they asked if Bill could do anything else that they should take into consideration.

Art replied, "He can understand every word that you are saying and as such he is wonderful at surveillance. Not only this, but he also can read as well as anyone that you know and has had police training in his previous life."

The voice came back, "Very good, give us a few minutes to consider all this."

It was an hour before they got back with Art and that too was part of the test to see just how they handled stress and being patient. Many an individual had failed this particular test, as their impatience usually led them to make derogatory remarks. Art and Bill just sat there and Art didn't say anything for the entire time. However, Bill was not as patient and was constantly relaying his thoughts to Art. Even though he was not very tolerant of this delay, he sat very still and didn't get down even once. The individuals watching were amazed and very pleased at the amount of control that this little Jack Russell had displayed. Then just at one hour, the mirror in front of them started sliding down into the floor and the whole wall was opening up to a much larger room full of people. Art fully expected the individuals sitting on the other side of that mirror to all be dressed in gray business suits and ties. Was he ever surprised to see the individuals dressed just as if they were on a shopping trip to the local mall. The women were in all manner of dresses and pants; while some of the men were even wearing shorts and flowered shirts.

One of the individuals, an older man dressed in an actual grey suit, stepped forward and said, "Welcome to our extremely eclectic group Art and you too Bill. You're welcome to refer to me as Mister Frank."

At this point Art was concerned with just what he had gotten them involved in; as these people didn't look like professionals at all.

The older man came up to Art, shook his hand he said, "Don't let looks fool you. The people in this room are among the smartest in the world in their fields. After all, what does a brainiac computer geek dress like anyway?

He took Art around the room, as they all knew him; but each of them required introductions to explain just what or who they actually were. At one point Art meet three women that were supposedly psychics. He was told that one could possibly dream about a crime, if she was allowed to study a particular crime long enough. Then he was introduced to one that had to come to the actual crime scene; to possibly see visions of that particular crime. Finally he was introduced to the third woman, who received visions from looking at or holding evidence from a crime. Art remembered what Don had told him, as he had heard of psychics before but didn't put much faith in them at all. Mister Frank told Art that in many cases their visions overlapped, but never contradicted each other. However, it wasn't every case that they were even able to help with. Then Art and Bill were introduced to a set of twins dressed in shorts and acting very strange. These two men had the uncanny ability of being able to read practically any crime scene and actually competed with each other to see who could come up with the most detailed information. Mister Frank confided in Art that he had wanted to strangle both of them on many occasions; but said that they are truly the best there is at what they do. Then Art met an Asian woman, who the older man told him was a living lie detector. Not like the machines which could be tricked or fooled by drugs; but an individual capable of monitoring all of a person's vital signs by simply holding onto their hand. He was introduced to three individuals that could absolutely do anything with a computer and no system was impervious to their access. In fact one in this group had been previously arrested for monitoring the Pentagon's computer system. With the knowledge this man received; he was able to do insider trading on companies that were to receive huge contracts from the military. The list of talent went on and on, with Art ending up utterly amazed. By the time that he had made it around the room; he didn't actually care how they dressed or what they even looked like. Most of them however seemed way more interested in Bill and tried their best to understand just how he could be Art's old partner.

A couple of times Bill told Art that he smelled Marijuana, but Art just ignored him. The older man asked Art for his key and gave him a thin metal bar about two inches long in return.

He said, "Next time come to the front door and touch this to the door knocker. The micro-charge within this alloy is adjusted to cause the door to open."

Almost instantly Art wanted to know when they could take a look at his case. He learned once more that they handle only one case at a time and they currently had three cases ahead of his. However, they asked that he submit everything about his case to them; where Mister Frank could evaluate it and place it next in line.

Then Mister Frank came up and said, "Art, you and Bill will receive a monthly stipend for as long as you are of service to us."

Art came back, "But I already have a full time job."

"Yes Art, and so do most of us, but we still get together and solve major crimes when asked to participate by the proper authorities," he replied.

"I'm guessing that these crimes could possibly be anywhere in the United States, right?" Art asked, "What about our expenses and how will I go about getting Bill there?"

Mister Frank spoke-up while handing Art a dull grey credit card with no writing on it, "Use this card for all of your expenses and they will all be taken care of. In most cases we will call you and ask you to show-up at a certain location. I can safely say that we will most likely be holding a crime scene for your arrival. We will book your flights for you and you will simply have to show-up at the gate and board the plane. If for some reason you should need to book a flight; then just book it in both of your names and everything will be alright when you present the card at the ticket counter."

That was a lot to take in for one day and on the road home Art wished that he had asked more questions. Bill wanted to know if he would be flying first class or in a kennel like the other dogs. Art wondered what Mister Frank meant when he said that they would be receiving a stipend monthly. When they finally arrived at home Sue Ann wanted to know everything about the meeting. Art told her that he guessed that it went alright, as they were now hired. Sue Ann instantly wanted to know what he meant by hired. After considerable discussion and explanation, Sue Ann understood most of what Art and Bill had been doing on this trip. She asked him several other questions, which he also didn't have the answers for. It was fairly evident that he should have taken her with him to negotiate everything; as she was somewhat of a hoot owl when it came to needing to know things.

When that first month's stipend just showed up mysteriously in their checking account; neither she nor Art had any further questions. Without notice ten thousand dollars had just appeared as if from nowhere, on a government transfer of funds. Art now knew that he needed to be prepared for when *The Gray Area* called for their services.

When Art arrived home from Baton Rouge with his incredible news; Sue Ann had temporarily forgotten that Don had already called three times earlier that same day. Each time he sounded almost frantic and asked her to have Art call him as soon as he got back. It was at this time that she remembered; just as the phone rang once again. Sure enough it was Don and he couldn't ask fast enough if Art and Bill had been accepted. He was very well pleased with their acceptance; until he heard that they were possibly fourth on the list of crimes that this group was presently considering. Finally he just congratulated Art and told him that he and Bill were now in the big leagues.

Chapter Sixteen

A few months ago Art had hit the end of his
rope with the mowing and knew that he desperately
needed to find a suitable person to handle this for him.
One of the local drunks, who they were constantly
handling, didn't have a job. Art took it upon himself to
offer this man a job mowing, with one major
stipulation; he had to show-up for work sober. Albert
Luna was tickled that someone would try to give him a
hand up and showed up at Art's home on his bicycle
almost daily. Art showed him how to care for and run
the zero turn mower, and Albert sat up there like he
was something. After he had been mowing for about
three weeks with no problems at all; Albert
approached Art and asked him if he might come
fishing sometime down there on his dock. This pleased
Art to see that Albert was getting some other interests
besides crawling inside a bottle; so he told him that he
could go fishing down there any time that he wished.
    Albert quickly came back, "I won't be bringen
no alcohol with me Mr. Art."
    Smiling and patting Albert on the back, Art said,
"Good, that's just what I wanted to hear."
    On parting, Albert asked, "What you thought
bout going fishen with me sometime Mr. Art?"
    "Yes I sure would," Art replied.
    Art had noticed that Albert was meticulous at
taking care of the mower and kept it looking almost
new. He was proud of what he had done for this
fellow human being and knew that he would be doing
even more in the future. The weeks had past and
several times Art had seen Albert down on the dock

fishing. Finally one beautiful evening, he told Sue Ann
that he was going down to do some fishing with
Albert. She was very pleased with this; as having
Albert around had slowed Art's drinking down also.
She smiled as she saw Art and Bill slowly easing down
towards the dock. By this time Albert already had four
catfish on a stringer and was patiently awaiting more.

Art asked, "Are they biting Albert?"

"Only in dhis here one spot, Mr. Art," he
replied. "I been fishen everywhere around dhis here
dock, but dhey only bite down here in dhis here one
spot."

Easing up next to Albert, he baited his hook and
dropped it in the water.

Albert said, "Watch here Mr. Art, ever so ofen a
speck of oil comes up from down dhere somewhere
and dhat's where dhe catfish like to bite."

Watching closely, Art noticed that in just a few
minutes a tiny droplet of oil came up from somewhere
down below and spread out to form a round circle on
the surface. Sure enough, at that particular moment a
fair sized catfish took his bait and the fight was on.
Albert was giving him instructions on how to land the
fish and all were excited, as even Bill was barking.
When Art finally got the fish up on the dock; he asked
Albert if he wanted it and that made Albert's day.
Several times Albert asked him if he was for sure and
then told Art just what a fine cook that his Ida Mae
was. He said that she could boil up some red beans
and rice, fry up that catfish, and it would just be
heavenly. After one more fish, Albert left out for home
and Art had thoroughly enjoyed himself this evening.
During the walk back up to the house he wondered if
Mr. Claybourn had ever enjoyed an evening here that
much.

About two weeks later Art received a call. The person instructed him to go to the airport and leave out on the very next Delta flight, immediately. He didn't know if he needed extra clothing or anything; but just decided to take Bill and go. He called Sue Ann along the way and she wished them her best. Art and Bill both weren't for sure what to expect when they arrived at the airport or just how that Bill would be flying. Upon arriving at the airport, he went straight to the Delta counter; where an airport security officer took him to the gate where his flight was being held. Driven right up to that gate, they were handed two first class tickets and he only supposed that Bill would be flying in a passenger seat next to his. The plane left out as soon as they were seated and not one question was asked about Bill from the flight attendants or the fact that Art was carrying a firearm. The passengers were quite another matter and Art just didn't know what to tell them. Finally he said that he had to pay one thousand dollars for his dog to fly first class and that silenced most of them. They now knew that their destination was Cleveland, Ohio; but nothing about what was to take place when they arrived. The woman that had called him actually didn't seem to know anything about what was even going on.

Coming off the plane with a small spotted dog following him, certainly narrowed the choices down rather quickly for the officer who was there to pick them up. This officer then lost no time at all in taking them straight to the crime scene; which was located about four miles outside the immediate city limits. Upon arrival Art saw a few faces that he now recognized; including Mister Frank who was coming straight towards him. Mister Frank informed him that they had preserved the crime scene for Bills nose to examine. It seems as though a white male about thirty years old had been found lying crumpled on the ground, just off the edge of the roadway. This killing fit the profile of the present case that *The Gray Area* was actively looking into in the Cleveland area. Without even being told, Bill put his nose to work and started across the area that had been roped off. The officer in charge of the scene started to try and stop Bill, but Mister Frank quickly intervened. Bill took his time and then after about twenty minutes he returned to make his report.

Art started in, "A car pulled off the road over here and male subjects got out of each front door. The one next to the road went around in front of the car for some reason and that was where he was shot. The other one stayed back, probably in the darkness and at some point took a leak. Most likely the one in the darkness was the one doing the shooting. Then the passenger walked around behind the car, entered the driver's door and left in what Bill believes was this man's car."

Mister Frank asked, "How sure is Bill that the passenger was a male? We've been working these killings for some time now and had it figured that the one doing the killing was a female."

Once more Art spoke-up, "Bill is insistent that the individual was a male alright. But from the smell of his urine he evidently is on estrogen to possibly make himself appear as a woman."

They marked the location of the urine to collect DNA samples and this was the first solid lead that they had to the individual's identity.

The group worked the crime scene for about four more hours and Bill was able to tell them that the dead man had not been with a female since his last shower. He also told them that he smelled beer and pizza around his face. At about that time the police informed Mister Frank that they had actually located the dead man's car. They all proceeded to that location and once more no one was allowed close until Bill had a chance to read the scene.

When Bill returned, Art started in, "The same male from out at the road got out of the driver's side of the car right here. Bill now says that he smells heavy makeup, hairspray, and possibly a permanent from the odor in the car."

Bill then took off around the car and across the parking lot. Art and the others were not far behind him. At one point he stopped at a footprint in the dirt and Art informed them that this print belonged to the man in question. They then continued on around the block to a pizza place and Art told them that there had been a second car parked right there. Only one person got into that car and he was also the man in question.

With just a little questioning, they found a girl that somewhat remembered the car sitting there as being one of those smaller SUVs, possibly gold colored. The twins came up with the theory of the man masquerading as a woman and working as a hairdresser. They also agreed that he or she had probably met the dead man at that particular pizza place and the plan was to go out to the country for sex. Art and Bill were released and spent the rest of that night headed back home. This was pretty wild, but kind of fun and they had both enjoyed the excitement. About a week later Art received another call and they had arrested the transvestite hairdresser that had as of that time killed eight men for no apparent reason at all. Art thoroughly enjoyed this new job, as there were no reports and no one wanted any record of their involvement.

Chapter Seventeen

      A few weeks later Art was busy with Karen on a local theft pandemic, when a solid lead finally came in which could possibly break the case wide open. The individual that stole the bike last night also stole a chainsaw at this same time. Chainsaws are notorious for leaking oil and the person ridding the bike away from the scene didn't realize that he was leaving a bread crumb trail, as such as it was. When the owner explained to Art and Karen what had happened; Bill was almost gone at that same instant.

      He had relayed to Art that he was trailing the oil from the chainsaw. They quickly returned to their vehicles and Art told Karen that they would follow Bill; who was now trailing the chainsaw. Neither Karen nor any of the other Officers had ever questioned Bill's interaction and found that on many of their cases he was invaluable. When Art wasn't just right there, Bill might bark or paw at something that he wanted brought to their attention and every time it seemed to be important. This particular day Bill was tracking the chainsaw and there was no question to that fact. Several times they had to stop and wait; as Bill had to back track and relocate the trail, when the bicycle rider made turns. Bill ran over twelve blocks before he finally turned off the street and proceeded past an old abandoned house. Art stayed right after him and Bill went through an opening in a fence; only to quickly return with the barking of a very large dog. He radioed Karen and told her which house that he was behind, so she promptly went straight up to the front of this house with her lights on. With the police now at the front door, the rats decided to abandon ship and quickly scattered out the back of the house.

Art was afraid that there might be several of them, so he stood at the back gate with a large canister of pepper spray. When they burst through the gate he started spraying each in turn. Now there were four young men on the ground and they were all screaming. Karen saw the individuals inside take off running; so she shoved the front door open and proceeded straight through what could have only been considered a flop house. In the middle of all of this the large dog came out and Art gave him a good dose of pepper spray as well. With four suspects now in hand, they had to summon additional help. Once they were all secured, Art found the house and back yard to be totally loaded with stolen items. The evidence gathering, cataloging and reports were going to take days to complete. With the suspects now safely in jail, Art and Karen could start cataloging everything with pictures.

Once back at the Police Department, Art and Karen were hard at it when Karen looked up and noticed that four rather strange looking people had walked in. She asked if she could help them and they said that they were looking for Art. Taking them to the door of the Chief's Office, Karen announced that there was someone there to see the Chief. He looked over their direction and immediately recognized Clare; as she always carried a gray purse out in front of her with both hands. Looking past her he recognized one of the other ladies and then the twins. His first instinct was to introduce them to Karen; but then he remembered that they had requested that they not be introduced to anyone.

Motioning for them to come in, Art said, "Step on in my office, as it is today."

There was evidence everywhere and he had to clear off his only two chairs for the two women to sit down.

Before he shut the door and locked it; he told Karen that he didn't know how long he would be and didn't want to be interrupted. With this she was left to do both of their jobs but never complained even once.

Art asked, "What is it that I have done that deserves such an illustrious visit."

Miriam, the other woman replied, "Mister Frank sent us to look at your case."

"But why, don't we only look at one case at a time," he asked?

"Yes, but Mister Frank feels that you're in grave danger and that changes everything," she remarked.

This really caught Art by surprise; as he already felt that he was in danger, but didn't realize that anyone else was even aware. He asked, "Just what's so special about Mister Frank that he was placed in charge and how would he know that I'm in danger?"

Clare spoke-up, "Mister Frank knows all and sees all."

Miriam was not at all amused by Clare's answer, so she replied, "He has a photographic memory, a computer for a brain and has the uncanny ability to feel what another person is feeling. He knew from that very first day that you felt you were in danger and now after studying your case he agrees. By now the murderer has weighed his options and has decided that this situation will not go away as long as you are involved."

Art knew that the stress between he and Ron had been steadily growing daily. Ron had stopped coming by the office during the day when Art was at work, and had even started wearing a vest. All of the officers were issued vests; but none wore them due to the high heat and humidity levels. Ron's now wearing a vest just indicated to Art that he was already contemplating his next move. From that very first day Art knew that there was something out there in the bay that had Ron's attention, but what? After several tries, Art finally found the new location where that Ron went each day to watch the bay. Searching the area and taking pictures; he was able to tell that Ron had a fairly clear view of his dock and boathouse for some reason, but an even better view of the back-bay area.

After reflecting on this situation briefly, Art asked, "Just where do we go from here?"

They told him that they needed to see all of the case files and evidence gathered from the two homicides. Art went out, and with Karen's help they carried all the evidence and case files into Art's already cluttered office. Karen now hoped to be included in just what was going on in there, but was just directed from the office once more by Art.

He followed her through the door and told her, "I'll fill you in later; but you know nothing about what is going on as far as anyone else is concerned, especially Ron."

This caught Karen totally by surprise and she immediately wondered what part Ron must have played in the two previous homicides. A chill ran up her back as she remembered the times that Ron had questioned her about Art and his looking into those homicides. A couple of hours later Karen was sent out for food and just happened to run into Ron at the dinner. Ron asked her who belonged to the black government suburban parked out in front of the Police Department, and she told him that it was just some of Art's old friends. This seemed to satisfy Ron's curiosity for the time being and he didn't ask anything about the homicides at that time.

Back at the office, Art had now gone through everything with the team and he could tell that their ideas were starting to flow. Once they were through with the two homicides; Art pulled out the death by natural causes of Mr. Claybourn. He told them that he was for sure that this was a third homicide, which had taken place at exactly this same time.

Clare held the tiny nitro bottle in her hand and it was evident that she was seeing something. She said, "From the first two cases I saw only the same vision twice. It was of a man in a boat out in the water fishing. But this time I saw a person using surgical gloves and they were placing some of these pills under a man's tongue."

Art told them of Ron and how he constantly watches the bay. He also told them that the officers all carry surgical gloves furnished by the local EMS. The twins put everything in prospective; as no one should have been with Mr. Claybourn at the time of his death. In fact his body was not even located for two days. At this time they visited the crime scenes; but people were already living in the two homicide victim's homes. Due to this all they could do was look at them from the outside. Miriam didn't feel anything looking at these scenes from so far off; but Art wanted her to go look at another location. He took them to his home and then on down to the dock.

He asked her, "Do you feel anything when you look out there?"

Miriam looked towards the dock and everyone could tell that she was seeing something. She walked back to where the others were standing and said, "I looked out towards the bay, but was distracted by a man in a boat. I believe that he was chopping holes in it with an axe. I couldn't see his face as I saw this from so far off." With this she pointed towards the house.

It was now very evident that Mr. Claybourn had seen something that got him killed. The team told Art that they would put their findings in a report and would forward it to him.

If Mr. Claybourn had seen something, then possibly did he report it to the local authorities? However, if he had noticed that the man doing this had just got out of a cop vehicle, then would he have actually called the Police? But if he hadn't called, then how would Ron have known what Mr. Claybourn had actually seen? Art proceeded to the office and started scouring through the old phone log books. Finally he found the book from the time in which Mr. Claybourn had died. Looking at the dates around that time he found no calls from the Claybourn residence. He was aware that the residence was out of the city limits, so he decided to make a call upon the County Sheriff. Sheriff Ladner was an older fellow and had been Sheriff of this county from even before time began. His office was very poorly funded and as such he had only two deputies. No officer ever remained there for very long; as the pay just never seemed to increase, after a shamefully low starting salary. This was part of why Sheriff Ladner had been there so long; as no one else was even remotely interested in his job. The Sheriff had no dispatch, so all of his phone calls were routed through the Police Department and were then relayed on to him. Art knew that the phone log reflected nothing for that time frame, but then Mr. Claybourn may have called the Sheriff directly. After visiting for almost two hours with the Sheriff, he learned only one bit of information that remotely fit in with this case. It would seem as though his records showed that his Deputy was dispatched to the Claybourn home on the day that Mr. Claybourn was found dead. It also reflected that Officer Fallon of the City PD volunteered to assist this Deputy on this call. Nothing was really unusual about this; as the Deputies were grossly inexperienced at best. In fact, to this very day it remained a constant policy for the City Officers to back-up the Deputies with any unusual calls that came in. The one thing that did strike Art as odd was that Ron had worked straight through for well over forty-eight hours at this time and then went in as soon as this call was handled. He definitely wanted an excuse for his DNA being at those scenes, if any should be found. Then on top of this he handled everything in such a manner that no real evidence was even collected. Ron definitely directed the Deputy into a call of natural causes, even before the local magistrate made it to that location.

Art decided that it was time to call Don and let him know exactly what all he had learned. Don was very interested in all of this, but felt that they weren't any closer than before with the proof side. This actually turned out to be the perfect time for Art to have called though; as the Senate was now through with their session for this year and Don was going to have some free time. Art told him of not locating a phone call from the residence and it sounded as if Don was almost excited. He told Art that he would be down there in two days and wanted him to have the phone log available for examination.

With this Art asked, "Did your father have a boat down there by the dock perchance?"

"Yes," Don replied. "It really wasn't much though, just an aluminum skiff with a rather old motor. I actually hadn't given it much thought, as it wasn't really worth anything."

"Well I think I know where it is," Art added.

That next day Art checked the old phone log out of evidence and knew that Ron would be coming in later. He worried about taking Karen into his confidence, but also worried about keeping things from her. Finally he made the decision to include her in this matter; as she had impressed him and he had tested her resolve to keep secrets on several occasions by this time. He asked her to come with him and they started patrolling the City, just so everything would look natural. He started in by telling her that what he was about to tell her, she could not breath a word of except in a court of law. She assured him that he could count on her and then Art told her that he knew who had committed the murders there in Bayoubay. Karen was quiet, but recalled Art telling the Mayor that he knew who the murderer was. Art started in explaining everything and then finally got around to Mr. Claybourn's death. By this time Karen was ready to say something and he could tell that she definitely needed a turn. He shut-up and she told him of the constant quizzing that she had taken from Ron; concerning Art's possibly looking into the murders. Karen relayed that she had told Ron that she knew nothing of the Chief investigating the murders and so far that had at least pacified him. Art told her not to change her story, but if Ron asked she could tell him that the Chief had sent the old phone log off for forensic analysis. Art knew that this would stir the waters even more and possibly shake Ron up to where he might make a move.

At about four that afternoon Don pulled up at Art's house and couldn't wait to get his hands on the old phone log. He had brought a pedestal camera and a forensic light with him. Carefully going over the pages just prior to receiving the dead body call from out at the Claybourn residence, he found exactly what he was looking for. Someone had used bleach and a toothpick to meticulously erase every word on this one call. Then they wrote over this same area to cleverly cover up what they had done. The call they replaced it with was a dog barking call, which showed to have been handled by Ron. It indicated what time he was supposedly dispatched, what time he arrived, and what time he completed the call. Everything there was false and there was a definite difference in the hand writing on this one call and all the others on this page. This was as close to a shred of evidence as they presently had. Art was well pleased; but Don said that it didn't prove anything about the murder of his father. They took several pictures of the light enhanced area and blew it up on the computer screen. They could read only a few of the words, and could see that the caller had asked for the Chief to return a call. Art got a cold chill at that time; as he wondered if the old Chief could have possibly been in on all this.

     Don agreed that this log needed to go to the State Crime Lab and he would drop it off by there himself the very next time that he was up in that area. After this they went outside with a couple beers, sat in the shadows, and watched the road leading into the place. Art brought up the fact that Ron was surely going to notice that the old phone log was now gone. Sure enough at about midnight, they saw a vehicle moving slowly along with no lights on and it eased to a stop at the bend in the road. The vehicle stayed there for over two hours and no one got out. Then they saw the back-up lights come on and the vehicle backed from whence it came. Art just figured that with Don's car there in the drive, Ron had lost his nerve. Don was very worried about his old friend at this point and really didn't want to leave him alone. After being reassured that Bill was on constant guard and the fact that Art now had his AR-15 at ready; Don felt at least a little at ease. They caught some sleep and woke up at about ten the next morning. Sue Ann had let them both sleep in; as after all Bill was definitely watching the grounds.

Art asked Don if he really wanted to stir things up today and Don allowed that he was ready. They purchased a long rope at the hardware store and attached a grappling hook to the end. Using Art's pickup truck, they backed it down beside the fishing dock. It didn't take hardly any trying at all before Art hooked something next to the dock in the water. They tied the rope to the back bumper of the truck and Art started pulling forward slowly. Whatever it was that they were hooked to, definitely seem to be moving towards them. Soon he heard Don shout that it was his father's old boat and motor. They continued on and pulled it completely out on the bank to where they could wash it down.

Art had already told Don of the vision, and the holes in the bottom were now readily evident.

Don said, "This is what caused my father's death. I just wish that he had called me before calling the police."

Art commented, "Help me get this on the trailer, I have a plan."

They slid the old boat and motor up on a flatbed trailer, and left out with their new find. Art took the whole mess to a boat dealership, and asked if they could find him the exact same boat and motor. This was a very odd request being that it was so old, but the man felt that he could surely find what Art was looking for. They then took the whole mess to a salvage yard and just gave it to them. Art asked Don to go ahead and take the phone log to the Crime Lab for analysis. They then meet Sue Ann at the house and Art wanted her to follow Don home. He didn't want her around for what would likely happen next. She was not in the least happy about this, but trusted that Art had everything under control. Art didn't let her know that he didn't really have anything under control; as far as this murder investigation was concerned.

Chapter Eighteen

With Sue Ann safely out of the picture, the boys
were just left to fend for themselves when it came to
meals. This wasn't even a topic that took much
discussion for the two of them; as they both thoroughly
loved good smoked pork ribs. Bayoubay had a place
located just outside the edge of town called, *Your Last
Stop*; which was basically a bar with a smoker going all
hours of the day and night. This place specialized in
the coldest beer around, but it was by far the pork ribs
off that smoker that kept everyone coming back. The
owner, Cal, never intended for his place to become a
restaurant and as such he furnished nothing else except
for the best lip smacking ribs around. Art would wait
until he was off work and then would take Bill with
him when he went in to gather up a side of Cal's ribs to
take home. Of course one good cold beer couldn't hurt
anyone and the patrons would have been thoroughly
put out if Art had acted as if he was too good to drink
with them. Art also took home a bottle of Cal's special
mopping sauce, but Bill just thought that it ruined the
flavor of the ribs. Bill was undoubtedly not a normal
dog and as such was not going to stand by quietly
while some one ate the meat off of the bones before
tossing them to him. No sir, he wanted fresh ribs, just
like Art did and ate until he could simply hold no
more. Being a dog, Bill might have had the intelligence
of a full grown man, but he still possessed the instincts
of a dog.

As a result, he would always pick up all the
bones and take them outside for proper placement. He
had carefully checked the place over and found no

better place than under the rather large fig tree, which was just outside Art's bedroom window.

While they were at *Your Last Stop* this one day; one of the patron's came over and asked Art if he could speak with him in private.

The man spoke-up, "You need to do something about that officer of yours."

"Which one, I have five officers," Art asked. Actually he knew that the man was surely going to say something about Ron; as he feared that Ron's attitude would naturally decline as they got deeper into this entire affair. He worried daily that something would actually surface to where he would have to let Ron go. Having his murder suspect tied to a job there in Bayoubay, kept him close and Art could find him if need be. One might argue that having him in a police car made him especially dangerous; but Art felt that the individuals in every car or truck he past was at least as well armed as his police officers.

The man didn't hesitate in openly mentioning Ron's name and Art got a lump in his throat. The man went on and told that Ron had mistreated a friend of his. No names were mentioned and at this point Art didn't push him for a name. Just as the man turned to walk away he said, "He also took his pistol."

That was just too much for Art to pass up, so he asked, "What kind of pistol was it?"

Stopping, the man turned and said, "A revolver, but just forget it. I've probably told you more than my friend would have anyway."

"An unregistered revolver, right," Art asked?

The man just shrugged his shoulders as he walked away. After this Art started worrying that Ron now had the weapon that he intended to use on him. In one sense it was a relief knowing that he would have to get in close to do the job. For several weeks now Art had worried that Ron might get a rifle and try to end things at a distance.

Art didn't drink much in the evenings these days; as he was always on call to backup the officers on duty. A thought ran through his mind that somehow Ron would call for backup and then lay a trap for him as he responded. Sure enough, Art was fast asleep this one night and received a call at about three in the morning. It was Ron and he said that he had just chased a burglar for about seven blocks, ending up at the old cotton warehouses. Ron asked him to hurry down to the east end; as he was presently following the man who had entered through the west end. These old cotton warehouses sprawled for about three city blocks and were like a maze of old junk piles inside. Art and Bill headed on down to the east end and there was no one around when they pulled up. The east end door was partially open and no one seemed to be in the area. Prior to this Art had purchased a military flak jacket to wear on just this type occasion and Ron wasn't aware of this. With his AR-15, urban assault rifle, at ready; Art started towards the partially opened door. When they were about half way there, Bill relayed to Art that someone was looking through the crack in the door.

With his rifle at his shoulder, Art shouted, "Come out with your hands in the air or die where you stand."

Ron was behind that door and had the revolver trained right on Art, but now realized that Art was wearing some sort of body armor. If that wasn't bad enough, Art had an AR-15 at ready and could return a devastating volley of fire in less than a second. There was no doubt in Ron's mind that his vest definitely would not withstand an AR-15 rifle round, much less several.

At this point he decided to cut his losses and hollered out to Art, "Hold your fire, it's me Ron."

When he came around the door, it was with a latex surgical glove on his gun hand and the pistol still being held tightly by the grip. Art kept his rife trained on him, but brought the stock down from his shoulder.

Ron asked, "Didn't you see him run past? He dropped his pistol back there and I recovered it for evidence." He noticed that Art still had his rifle on him so he stopped.

Without taking the rifle off him, Art asked, "Have you made that pistol safe yet?"

Looking down at the pistol, Ron pushed forward with his thumb and the cylinder fell open. Then in one swift motion, he raised the pistol and dropped the bullets into his ungloved hand.

Art commented, "Thanks for preserving the finger print evidence on those bullets."

Smiling something evil like, Ron replied, "Sorry, I'll try to do better next time."

With the loaded pistol now made safe, Art slowly moved his rifle slightly off of Ron.

Ron spoke-up, "I'll take this pistol back and process it for finger prints, possibly we'll get lucky there."

As Art watched him just slowly walk away, he had the almost uncontrollable urge to just shoot him in the back. It was incredibly sad when an officer absolutely knew what had happened; but there was not enough evidence to prove anything. Art had been in this same position several times before and more than not justice was never served.

A few days later Art received a phone call from Mister Frank. At first he thought that he might have to drop everything and go wherever it was that they needed his help; but this time it was Art that was receiving the help. Mister Frank told him that Martha had now experienced a few visions and possibly they had something that could finally help him.

It would appear that Martha's first vision was of some sort of Satanic Cult. She didn't make much of this, but soon she received a second vision of two individuals bringing gold coins through a hole in a wall. The two men were then dropping them into stainless steel beer barrels. Then the third vision came of a man with his head and hands missing.

Having these visions after studying his homicides brought Art to conclude that somewhere out there in the bay were the beer barrels with the gold coins inside.

Mister Frank told Art that they were looking into this matter as they spoke and he would get back with him as soon as they had more information. Art was not aware of this fourth man's death and now strongly felt that Ron had four individuals he was directly responsible for killing. With this many deaths already attributable to his credit; Ron would not hesitate in killing again. Mister Frank wanted to know if he could send some people to help with security there and Art told him that he didn't want that at this point. These days Art and Bill would stay up until about two in the morning, as Ron had pulled down the driveway several times. What they didn't know was that Ron was well aware that he was keeping them up late on purpose.

A few more days past, and Art and Bill were once more fast asleep. It was getting towards morning and Bill heard something. He was a very light sleeper and many times at night he would ease out the doggie door to take a look around. Several times he had seen Ron pull down the driveway and knew well what his vehicle sounded like. This night however he hadn't heard any vehicles, but rather something moving about outside. In the past he had found wild pigs, deer, and even stray livestock wandering about the property. On this particular night the sound was coming from the far side of the house.

There were several bushes and plants around the house, which allowed Bill to move about without being noticed. Upon coming in close to the large fig tree, he suddenly smelled Ron. Easing in closer; he could see that Ron was backed into the limbs of the fig tree and was fairly well hidden. He had a revolver in his gloved hand and was totally concentrating on the bedroom window. Then Bill faintly heard something else up under that same tree and moved around to see just what it was. This old fig tree was massive and came clean down to the ground to cover an area equal to two cars parked side by side. This time the sound was coming from where Bill had hidden the rib bones and he was almost on them before he realized what was happening. Suddenly, directly in front of Bill was a family of skunks and all he could think to do was start barking. That fig tree totally exploded with the most ungodly odor and Bill went to rubbing his face all over the ground. He knew that Ron had run from that location, but to just where he didn't know. As quickly as Bill was able; he ran around back and straight in through the doggie door. Bill came down the hall barking to warn Art and Art jumped out of bed to the horrible odor of skunk. He turned on the bedroom light and Bill instantly started instructing him to kill the light because Ron was out there somewhere. Quickly turning off the light, Art grabbed Bill and headed straight for the shower. He turned on the cold water, practically threw Bill inside and instantly went back for his rifle. Bill didn't even care that the water was cold; as his eyes and nose were burning profusely

at that time. It was still dark outside, so Art couldn't
see much as he slipped around the inside of the house.
Coming back in to where Bill was; Art turned the water
off and asked him to remain there. With this
everything was put on hold, until the sun came up
enough to see exactly what was going on outside. Art
slipped around outside and found the location of last
night's fiasco. He followed Ron's footsteps for as far as
he could and saw where they headed off into the
woods. Back in the house, Art knew that he would
have to bathe Bill in tomato juice to kill the skunk odor.
He went to the pantry and all he could find was a large
jar of garlic, onion, basil, spaghetti sauce. He took this
jar and climbed right in the shower with Bill, clothes
and all. The spaghetti sauce was rather thick, but
spread easily over Bill's short hair. Then Art started
thoroughly working it in from the tip of his tail to the
end of his nose. By this time Bill was licking the
tomato sauce off and thought that it wasn't half bad.
Art looked at his buddy and now Bill was a rather
bright shade of orange. In fact it took two washing
with soap to remove most of the orange color. They
dried off and were setting on the edge of the bed
discussing what all would have to be done to the
house, when Art received a call from Mister Frank. He
told Art to once more go to the airport, as they were
needed this very moment. There was no such thing as
discussing issues with Mister Frank and he hung up
before Art could even get a word in sideways. Art
quickly got dressed and the two of them took off for
the airport. On the way there he called Karen and told
her that he was called away rather quickly. He asked
her if she would mind getting someone to come in and
take care of the skunk problem.

He didn't tell her about Ron being there, but
rather of his having to wash Bill in spaghetti sauce.

Karen got a good laugh and said that she would find someone to handle this situation.

When Art and Bill arrived at the airport, they were immediately confronted with a dilemma. Several of the airline personnel strongly felt that they couldn't fly with that odor on them and phone calls were quickly being made. Sure enough, they were thanked for their concern, but soon learned that Art and Bill had to be on that particular flight.

This was one flight where there were no questions about Bill flying as a passenger and they didn't make any new friends at all. Once they arrived in Atlanta, the officer picking them up couldn't believe how bad they smelled. Art had a hard time believing just how bad they smelled after bathing for almost an hour. He took them to the crime scene, which was located in one of the better additions and there was a huge home with cars all out in front of it. Art and Bill waited outside patiently for Mister Frank to come to them.

As he was walking up, he suddenly stopped and asked, "What happened to you two?"

With his head hung low, Art replied, "Bill had a slight run-in with a skunk and we were in the process of cleaning him up when you called."

"Well, let's not contaminate the crime scene any more than it already is," he remarked. "You two get a room and see if you can do something about that odor."

They checked into a very nice hotel and ordered ten gallons of tomato juice and a gallon of vinegar. Art rolled all of his clothes up and placed them in a bag for cleaning.

Art and Bill both climbed into the tub filled with the tomato juice and vinegar. Bill thought that this was pushing togetherness to the fullest extent. It took some convincing from Art, but Bill finally snorted some of the vinegar water up his nose. This just led to sneezing fits and his nose had to be thoroughly rinsed out with water. On the way there that day Bill kept telling Art that his nose didn't work and they would just be making a fool of themselves by even showing up. That following morning Bill could smell bacon cooking and immediately wanted to go looking for it. They then had a hardy breakfast and proceeded back to the crime scene.

Mister Frank met them once more and filled them in, "We are looking for one or more individuals that are kidnapping rich people's children. They were active at Charleston, moved to Nashville and now are operating out of Atlanta. They have kidnapped both male and female children; have not molested any, but they have killed some. The big difference in this case is the fact that this child was insured for ten million dollars. We don't know if this was a ploy to make money or just a caring parent.

However, we have learned that the mother is being treated for postpartum depression and the father is the one who really has the money. My question to everyone is whether or not this is actually part of the kidnappings that we are already working or not?"

Art and Bill were shown around the house and to this point the mother was still sticking with her story. She claimed that someone had come in and took the two year old girl. With a through pass through of the house, the father threw a fit. He demanded to know just why a dog was being allowed to roam free through his home. Bill was standing there at that time and told Art that the father had been with a woman recently, who was not his wife. They settled the father down and told him that Bill was reading just who had been in their home. They didn't want to proceed any further with this conversation and no one knew just how that Bill relayed his information to the ones investigating the case. On a subsequent debriefing, Art told Mister Frank that both the mother and father had been with different partners recently; but that didn't mean that they were involved in the kidnapping or cover-up. Bill found other odors in the house and that meant that possibly someone else had been there. They planted tracking devices on the two parent's cars and told them that they were closing everything out for the day. The parents weren't showing any closeness at all and it was evident that they wouldn't have planned this together. In the past cases, the kidnapper had contacted the family on the third day and they felt that this would be the situation this time also. Whether it would be the real serial kidnapper or just a scam pulled by one of the parents; they were just for sure that this same schedule would actually be followed. That evening both parents headed out in their respective vehicles and both took different routes. Mister Frank agreed with the twins that the little girl would probably be kept alive until the ransom was paid. The clock was ticking and every lead needed to be followed up on in very quick order.

The father's car was the first to come to rest. Art and Bill were dispatched to that location, to see what Bill's nose could possibly tell them. It just so happened that it was at the home of one of this man's secretaries; as they had been having an affair ever since his wife became pregnant. This showed little concern for his family and possibly his own daughter. So why then would he purchase a ten million dollar policy on his child? With this man just randomly taking out this huge policy on his daughter; he could easily be cutting ties with his wife and at the same time making a profit. Art and Bill arrived at this location and immediately

Bill went to work. In no time at all he reported back that there were no indications that the little girl had ever been there. Going up to the door, they rang the door bell and were soon confronted by the father and his mistress. He was furious at their insistence that they be allowed to search the house. However he soon settled down, when he was told that this could possibly eliminate him as a suspect, in the event that his daughter was found dead. This actually was not a good sign and made them feel that the father felt that the little girl would actually be found dead. Mister Frank confronted him directly about this and he finally admitted that he felt that his wife had been the one that took the girl. He showed a definite lack of concern and they then learned that he was well aware that he wasn't the little girl's father. This man had undergone a vasectomy early in life, as he didn't want children, but had not told his wife about this situation. However, he did admit that he felt that his wife would end up doing something to the child and there was no reason that he should not make a profit on this whole mess.

It was at this time that the wife's car finally came to rest. She had driven all over town in a definite effort to shake any tails that were following her. Finally she ended up at a motel only about ten blocks from their home. The authorities felt that she must surely be the one responsible for the missing little girl and chose not to push in too quickly. Bill however was dispatched to survey the area and came back with what possibly could be good news. His nose had hit on the scent of the little girl at the door to one of the rooms, but was she still there? Everyone stood down until the mother left three hours later. Then they moved in and found her boyfriend, but he was now alone.

Back at the home that next day, neither of the parents was aware of what had happened to the other and now just waited for the fateful phone call. True to form, the kidnapper on the morning of the third day once again asked for one million dollars. This time however the money drop was not anywhere near as elaborate as it had been in the past. The father, with a new guilty conscious, agreed to make the payment and earnestly hoped that the little girl could be returned safely.

Everything was put into play and then one of the women had a vision. The vision showed a woman picking the little girl up there in the house and the girl didn't even seem to be scared. Quickly the twins came to the same conclusion; that this woman could actually have been hired help.

With a quick list of everyone that had recently worked for them in hand, Art and Bill set out. They would look into the female employees first, as it had been a woman who took the little girl from the house. Success came at the second house they checked. The woman that lived here had came in and done the wife's nails recently; she felt that this family would be perfect for a visit from the kidnapper. Bill had hit on the little girls scent almost instantly and quickly located a direction that she had been taken. The residence was secured and everyone was following Bill. He proceeded around back and in a locked shed he located the little girl. She was alive, but not in good shape at all.

Mister Frank picked up on the fact that she was totally taped-up with black electrical tape. No one had released the fact that the kidnappers had taped their victims up with that type of tape to anyone. He also fairly well knew now just why that some were released alive and others were found dead. With the victims taped up in such a manner as this, some had simply expired prior to the ransom being paid. However, prior to this point none of the victims had actually seen the individual who took them and this little girl had; or at least that was the way it was seen in the vision. Possibly the ones who had seen their kidnapper were simply allowed to expire on purpose. Rather quickly, the woman who lived here wanted to strike-up a deal with them. Only after everyone was certain that the little girl would actually live, did the authorities give credence to any sort of a deal. But just what was it that this woman thought she had, which could possibly be used to help her. As it turned out, she and a few of her girlfriends in nail school had talked about and came up with the entire kidnapping scheme. They each went their separate way after the school was over and nothing came of it; but then about two years later the kidnappings began. She just knew that it had to be one of the other girls, but had said nothing about this to the authorities. Then after several kidnappings happened in various cities; she got the grand idea to do one of these herself. She even told them that the girls had talked about using the black electrical tape to secure the children. Not only that but each had also talked about giving a date rape drug to the child; so that they would have no memory of who took them. Now it made perfect sense and a list was compiled of all the women who had plotted this whole thing out so many years before.

Chapter Nineteen

Art returned home to find a house that definitely smelled a lot better than when he left it. Karen had done a wonderful job at getting everything cleaned up and had even taken care of the skunk problem. Very few skunks were ever seen around there and now there were a few less. She told Art that Ron showed up the next day after he left and wanted to know just what she was doing. She explained to Ron that she was taking care of a problem for the Chief, since he was called out of town rather abruptly. Ron had also hit her up about where the Chief had gone, what he was doing and when he would be back. Of course she didn't really have an answer for any of these questions and that didn't seem to set well with Ron.

That following week a call came in concerning a missing three year old girl right there in Bayoubay. Art took the initial call and everyone was called in to help. Karen entered the child in the Amber Alert System and started gathering evidence. Art gathered up Bill and they headed straight over to the house where the child was missing from. The mother was hysterical and totally blamed herself for taking her eyes off of the child, if even only for a short period of time. They acquired some items that belonged to the child and Bill caught the little girls scent. Bill and Art circled the block three times and not once did Bill cut across the little girl's scent trail. This was not a good sign, as it meant that she was ether still there somewhere or someone had taken her. Looking at the house, one thing was for sure, there would be no ransom call. Quickly narrowing their search, Bill didn't even locate

the scent of the little girl leaving that immediate
property. However, on that property her scent was
everywhere. The house was up on blocks, so Bill went
all over underneath it without hitting on anything.
This was not a good situation; as most of these type
kidnappings ended up in a shallow grave. Room by
room Art and Bill went throughout the entire small
house and checked every space where a tiny girl could
possibly be hiding. At one point Karen came up to
where Art was located and told him that even though
he had been called in, Ron just chose to not help with
this matter. Art knew that it was rather flagrant for
Ron to just ignore a call like this and he also knew that
Ron had left work at about midnight last night. By this
time he should've had plenty of sleep, if that was truly
what he was doing. Art worried that Ron might have
been out moving the gold last night and had not slept
at all. Not being able to share with everyone that the
little girl had not just wandered off; Art had to mount
an all out search for her in the community. By this time
It was getting late in the evening and everyone was
fairly tired; so Art told a few of the searchers to go
home for the evening. On his drive to the house he
thought of just how good a cold beer would be at this
time and almost couldn't wait to unwind. He hoped
that he wouldn't turn the corner just to see Ron sitting
there at his home. When he finally did turn the corner,
he didn't see a vehicle, but did see a subject just sitting
down on the dock. Going to the house first, he took his
binoculars and could easily tell that it was Albert. He
had evidently come over to try his luck at fishing once
more. Art sure wanted a beer in the worst way, but not
around Albert; as he had been doing so well since Art
gave him the job mowing. He decided to walk on
down to where Albert was sitting and thought that he
might as well take his pole along.

Upon reaching the dock, Albert commented, "You been worken entirely too much Mr. Art."

Art replied, "Your right Albert, but today we were searching for a missing little girl."

Jerking his head around, Albert said, "You ain't talken bout dhat dhere Taylor girl is you Mr. Art?"

"Why yes Albert," Art replied. "Do you know anything about that little girl or where she might be?"

"I sure does Mr. Art. I was moseyen along dhere dhis here mornen and saw her mother come runnen out dhe house like she was all in a hurry. She was still putten her shirt on and definitely had nothen under it. She jumped in her car and started back before dhe car was even goen. Dhat little girl, she was a playen out dhere by dhe driveway. Her mother was in such a hurry dhat she almost backed over her. Dhat car did knock dhe little girl down dhough. She was hit by dhe front of dhe car when it swung out. When I got dhere dhat girl was cryen something awful. By dhis time dhe mother was way on down dhe road. I picked dhe little girl up and took her to dhe house. Dhe door was standing wide open. I called out but no one came to dhe door. Mr. Art, I took dhat little girl over to my house and gave her to Ida May to care for. Ida May told me dhat dhe mother don't deserve dhat child. She said dhe mother was probably doen drugs and just needed to worry about dhis for a day or two. I left out after dhat and came out here to start mowen. Dhe little girl, she must still be dhere with my Ida May."

Picking up his cell phone, Art called Karen and told her everything. She said that she would handle it from her end, but would sometime need a statement from Albert. Art asked if she had seen Ron and she said that he had at least clocked in at 6 o'clock.

The two men went to fishing and Art told Albert about finding the old fishing boat sunk right where the oil spots were coming to the surface. He told him about finding the holes chopped in the bottom and the fact that he was getting another boat just like the old one.

Albert commented, "Dhen dhat's why I ain't had no luck in dhis here spot. Say Mr. Art, what you think of taken me out fishen in your new boat when you get it?"

"Well I guess we could go out sometime Albert. I just hadn't really thought about what I was going to do with it," Art remarked.

"Dhen why you gitten one Mr. Art," Albert asked?

"Well I guess I just bought it to replace the one that was damaged," Art replied.

He couldn't tell Albert what he really needed it for, or even who had damaged the old boat.

Albert spoke-up after a bit, "I can show you where dhe big ones are Mr. Art. I been out dhere with Mr. Hewitt and with Mr. Rheims several times."

"Did they take you out there in Mr. Claybourn's old boat," Art asked?

"Yes sir, right here from dhis here dock. Mr. Claybourn, he was a good man and let Mr. Hewitt and Mr. Rheims both use his boat."

That was exactly what Art had been looking for. Now he had the common thread that tied all three men together into a triple homicide.

He told Albert, "I have something real important to take care of and then someday we can go out there fishing." Art asked Albert just where the good fishing was located and Albert tried his best to show him where the two men had taken him.

That very next day, Art went to check on the progress of finding the exact boat that had been damaged. The man at the marina took him to look at one that was almost exactly the same and even had a very similar old motor. They haggled with the owner for a little bit and the man even started the motor to show them just how good a shape that it was in. Art made a point of dragging the boat around town for all to see, in hopes that the word would get back to Ron. He wondered what had happened to Don, as he surely should have been back here by this time. When Art passed by Karen, she waved him over and said that he sure needed to return a call to a man named Mister Frank. Sure enough, Art had left his cell phone at home today and really thought he would be back before now. He headed out to his place and as soon as he turned the bend, he saw Sue Ann's car parked in its usual place. Pulling up beside the house, he hoped that it would be Don that he saw. A great sigh of relief came over him when he saw Don sitting out on the porch in the area that his father use to enjoy.

He told Art, "I don't know why that you left that damnable phone here, but it has been absolutely about to ring itself to death."

Art went in, gathered up two beers for them and picked up his cell phone. He headed out to the porch and could see that the most of the calls had come from Mister Frank. Returning a call finally, Mr. Frank was distressed but very pleased to hear Art's voice. He told him that he had already placed a call to get Art some security and it was coming like it or not. Art had to do some tall talking to get everything called off and convince Mr. Frank that he needed only a few more days before everything would come together. Mister Frank told Art that Martha had one more vision and it was of Ron standing over him, in the dark, with a pistol in his hand. This sent cold chills up Art's back, but at least he knew what was coming. He had been constantly worried that Ron might get a high powered rifle and try ending this at a long distance, especially since he had started carrying the AR-15. In Mississippi this is usually not possible, due to the underbrush, except that is over water. Art knew that from Ron's new viewing location, he could easily see the boat dock area.

Then Mister Frank passed on to Art what all they had learned about the gold. He said that a satanic cult down near El Paso, Texas had defrauded their followers out of millions and had changed all of this money into gold Krugerrands. It would seem as though they didn't trust banks and didn't want to have to explain where all this money came from. They also didn't trust the government and didn't want it tied up in good old US currency. Sure enough, when they had amassed somewhere near six million dollars, they had a major falling out. Several graves were found out in the desert and the gold had mysteriously disappeared. When the authorities started checking into the headless man; they found that he belonged to the original group and was supposedly thought to be among the survivors of the falling out. From what they had learned, the gold and several other items taken during the falling out were hidden in a storage building in San Angelo, Texas. However, about four months later the headless man left the group and the gold mysteriously disappeared at about this same time. The gold it seems was taken by the headless man renting the storage unit directly behind the one with the gold in it. He and a friend cut a hole in the wall between the two storage units and removed the gold. From what Martha saw, the gold coins were placed in stainless steel beer barrels to be carried away. Mister Frank then told him that they didn't have the slightest idea why this man was killed, or why his head and hands were missing. At first it was thought that some of the ones in the cult had caught up with him; as this was their signature work. However, with all this information in hand, a comparison had now been made between his DNA and that of Ronnie Fallon. Comparing the two, they were now pretty sure that the dead man was actually a cousin to Officer Fallon.

Art thanked him for all the information and told him that he had a buddy looking out for his safety at this time. Mister Frank told him that he would give him and Don one week and then he was sending him security, whether he wanted it or not. Clare had said that Mister Frank knows all and now Art was getting a taste of this; by Mr. Frank's knowing that Don was the one there helping him. Art had a lot to do now, which should push everything to a certain and fairly final end. For one thing he and Don took the boat down and tried it out. The boat worked fine and fairly quickly Art felt comfortable in operating it. He then called Karen and told her to subtly break it to Ron that he knew who the murder was and should have enough information by next week to make an arrest. Don had been requested to bring a high powered surveillance wire with him and he had. This was so that Art could be wired in preparation for his meeting with Ron. A few days before the plan was actually placed into action; Art took Karen to a road near his place and from there she could see if a vehicle turned down his road. He also had everything setup to where she could listen in on his and Ron's conversation. In this manner she could hear every word that was being said and could record everything. Karen would be the perfect witness in a courtroom; as she articulated everything extremely well.

The morning of the set-up, Art and Don went over everything and then shook on their plan. They had a ton of circumstantial evidence, but very little on Ron himself.

There would be no way to make an arrest without a full confession. At about two in the evening Art took his fishing gear and climbed into the old boat. He went out to where Albert had told him that the big fish were located; but he was way more interested in looking for anything that would indicate that something was out there. He jigged up and down with a heavy lead jig containing two sets of treble hooks for hours and constantly moved around. Finally in about twenty feet of water he hung something, but it was just too much for his twenty pound test line; so as a result he just kept breaking the jigs off. Art hoped that by dusk, surely Ron would notice what he was doing and would have to come confront him. The sun was quickly setting; as Art slowly started back across the bay. He watched his landing, with great anxiety, for as long as he possibly could. A heavy fog was rolling in across the bay and darkness was pushing in hard. By the time that he arrived at the dock, it was almost totally dark and the light from the house was very dim in the fog. It was a moonlit night but the heavy cloud cover had almost totally excluded any sign of the moon. When he finally saw the dock; a cold chill run across his back thinking that Ron was probably out there in the dark somewhere in front of him.

Art was just getting prepared to tie-off to the dock; when he heard a voice from somewhere out in the darkness. Looking up he held his hand up to block out what little light was coming from the house, but still couldn't make out who was speaking. However, without even seeing the individual, he knew it was Ron.

Ron spoke-up, "Art, just don't do anything stupid."

This day Art had worn shorts and a T-shirt, so anyone looking could see that he wasn't carrying a gun or wearing a vest. He stood very still and said, "Is that you Ron?"

"Who else were you expecting? Karen told me that you were ready to make an arrest on the homicides next week and I just couldn't let that happen," Ron replied.

"Yes, on all three of them," Art added. "But why Mr. Claybourn?"

Ron replied, "He wasn't supposed to be at home. I had no intentions of hurting him. But he just came back from the hospital too soon."

"Yes, you had to do something to keep everyone from going out there where the gold is located didn't you?"

Ron then moved closer down the dock and asked, "Just how did you know about the gold?"

Art commented, "That's why you killed Tom and Winston wasn't it?"

"That gold just makes a person paranoid," he replied. "I should have never got involved with it from the first. I looked out there one day and saw Tom fishing right over the spot where the gold was hidden. At that moment I knew that I needed to do something about Tom. The day that I killed him, I came back to this very spot to destroy the boat and it was gone. Looking out on the bay, I saw someone else fishing right over the gold once more. It was Winston and I had to stop him also. That very next day I took care of him and returned to take care of the boat. Mr. Claybourn had been in the hospital having multiple heart bypasses. He wasn't expected to be home for another month, if he even came home at all. Was I ever surprised to read the phone log and see that he had called to talk with the Chief. I knew instantly what he had seen and I couldn't let him tell anyone. It was very simple; I found him sleeping on the porch, walked up behind him and put a rag filled with chloroform over his face. Once he passed out, I just opened his nitro bottle and poured them out on the table there in front of him. At that point I put nitro pills under his tongue until he finally had a heart attack and died. Then at that point I worked straight through for almost three days, until the call came in of his death. I quickly volunteered to help the County Deputy and he was easily duped into just what I wanted him to believe. But enough of this, I need for you to restart that motor and we'll take us a trip across the bay."

"What if I refuse," Art asked?

Ron quickly added, "If I have to shoot you right here, I'll undoubtedly have to kill Sue Ann also. But if I do you across the bay; then I shouldn't have to do anything to Sue Ann, but console her for her loss. Besides, I need to send this damnable boat to the bottom once more, where it won't ever be found. So don't you try anything foolish and get that motor going again."

"You mean that you're not interested in knowing who else knows about the gold out there in the beer barrels," Art asked.

"Just how did you know about the gold and the barrels anyway," he asked.

"Well actually it was from finding your cousin, the way you left him," Art remarked.

"I tried to make it look like those goofy Satanists that he ran with had killed him. How exactly did you figure it out anyway," Ron asked?

"From a DNA comparison were you just happened to show up as his cousin," Art replied.

"Oh yes, the DNA that I furnished on this case to rule me out. That's ironical that it was actually what ruled me in," he remarked.

"Yes, and then it was very simple to figure out that you had hidden the beer barrels, with the gold coins inside, right out there in the bay."

"Would you believe that I hid the gold right in the very spot where those old men had baited a fishing hole? I just couldn't let them fish there anymore; they would have spoiled everything," Ron added. "Now get that motor started or we can do it right here and I can deal with Sue Ann also."

"Ron you don't want to do this, because when they find my body they'll know that I was murdered," Art pled.

Just pointing the pistol at Art, he said, "No, they won't find anything. I've been feeding a bull gator out there that's about fourteen feet long and he'll eat anything that starts rotting out there in the water. I once even saw him take down and carry off a full grown deer."

"Say, isn't that the same pistol that you were pointing at me the other night at the cotton warehouse," Art asked?

"Yes it is," he replied, "I was planning on doing this that night, until you showed up in that fancy vest you were wearing."

"Then I guess that it might even smell like skunk, right," Art inquired?

"That's right one more time, but it's a shame that you outsmarted yourself by going out there in this old boat."

With everything now said; Karen activated her lights and siren, and here she came. Even in this heavy fog, the darkness was abruptly disrupted and Ron was definitely in distress.

About this time Don shouted, "Art, watch out!"

Then Bill started barking from the opposite side of the dock.

Ron spun around to meet this new threat; but Don was carefully hidden just inside the old boat house and Bill was hidden behind a tree. As Ron's gun came off of Art, Art reached quickly for his own pistol; which just happened to be conveniently leaned up behind his tackle box. Ron couldn't see anyone out in the darkness and was quickly turning his attention back to Art's sudden movements. Then suddenly from the darkness of the boat house, Art's AR-15 ran-out and the muzzle blast momentarily disrupted the total darkness. The impact caught Ron in the center of the vest like a bat swung by a professional baseball player. There has never been a vest made that could stop an AR-15 round and Ron tumbled off the far side of the dock. Art had his pistol at ready by this time; but there was no need for it, as Ron's body lay motionless face down in the water.

Art could tell that Karen was trying to kill herself getting there, so he spoke-up, "Slow down Karen, it's over."Still she arrived at about the same time that Don made it over from the boat house. Before they did anything further, Art called the Mayor. He told him that they had just killed the town's murderer out at his house and he was needed out there as soon as possible. Art's second call was to Mister Frank. He told him that it was finally over and that Officer Ronnie Fallon was now deceased.

Mister Frank remarked, "Good, then I will mark this case closed and we can get on with the business at hand." Then he asked, "He didn't tell you where he hid the gold, did he?"

Art replied, "Yes, as a matter of fact he told us that the gold was at the bottom of the bay and is being guarded by a fourteen foot gator."

"Well good luck finding it and I just know that you'll do something special with it when you do," he commented. "Watch out for that gator."

Karen asked, "Where did the gold come from?"

"That's a long story Karen and I'll tell it to you sometime while were searching for it. The Red Cross sure does a lot of good for a lot of folks; it's time that someone did something good for them," Art remarked.

The Mayor finally arrived and there was one of his officers in uniform laying dead, where they had drug him up on the bank. The mayor looked confused and not at all happy about what he was seeing.

Art quickly said, "Karen let him listen to the recording."

After listening to the recording, the Mayor came back over and shook Art's hand.

"I would have never believed that Ron could have possibly done all of that." He looked over at Don and said, "You were right all along and I just didn't want to believe what you were saying." Then the Mayor said, "I'll need to set up a news conference and tell the world that our Chief, Art Jankowski, has finally killed the town's murderer.

Art spoke-up once more, "No, you better tell them that Senator Claybourn saved your Chief's life by killing the town's stalker. He had already killed four times that we know of, and was planning on killing me and my wife."

When the news went out, it went nationwide and caused Don to not only be an easy reelection, but gave him illusions of becoming the next US Senator from Mississippi. Art finally found a replacement for Ron, and then broke it to the Mayor that he also needed a replacement for the Chief's position. The money that *The Gray Area* had been paying Art had built up in his account; to the point where he really no longer needed to work for a living. He did however purchase himself a much better boat. It was in fact a top of the line deck boat. Art and Karen borrowed a salvage barge and went looking for the gold. That day out there jigging he had lost four jigs by hooking something in one area and it turned out to be the beer barrels that were all tied together with nylon roping. They carried them ashore and that weekend Don was also there. Don took the gold Krugerrands and went around the State to all of the Red Cross Offices. In each office he left off their share. True to his nature he also used this to deliver a carefully structured political speech at this same time. This too made the news, but Don told them that the gold had came in to his office from an anonymous donor; with specifications that it be shared between all the Red Cross Offices within the State. With the gold now thoroughly and publicly distributed; the ones that would be looking for it could give up on their search. However, word got around the City of Bayoubay that it was actually pirates gold and there could be much more hidden out there somewhere in the bay.

Art didn't really have a lot of use for the old boat anymore and told Albert that he was making him a gift of the boat. Albert had never been given anything this nice in his whole life and started crying. Art told him that he could keep it at the new dock that he was going to build, for as long as he liked.

Bill had not played much of a part in the closing of this case, but without him they would not have gotten as far as they had. Art was now ready for things to slow down a bit, but was also ready at a moment's notice, just in case *The Gray Area* should call.

Chapter Twenty

It all sounded like a very slow paced and laid back retirement, but it was anything but that. The Mayor made Art promise him that he would avail himself to help the Department with any future cases and Art agreed. Karen was a very sharp person and picked up on the fact that a good portion of Art's abilities came from Bill. She just knew that somehow Art could understand this small dog, but Art never told her how it worked. The next two Chief's both suffered ego problems in consulting with Art and as a result just did not last. One of them had even wanted to run all the officers off and start over; simply because they spoke too much about how Art had done things. Needless to say, the Mayor intervened and once more they were looking for a Chief. Each time they found themselves without a Chief; the Mayor would go out to Art's and totally beg him to take the position back. Finally Art told the Mayor that he would take the position back as an unpaid position; only if he could appoint an Assistant Chief to draw the pay and carryout the day to day duties of the office. The Mayor was very pleased with this situation; as it tied Art to the department, gave it some stability and added one additional person to the staff. The next City Council meeting Art showed up and announced that he was appointing Karen to the position of Assistant Chief and they would have to start looking for a new evidence officer. Everyone was very quiet and no one wanted to give their approval at this time. As Art was leaving, he told the mayor that they could approve his request or start looking for a Chief. However, he wanted them to know that if they didn't approve his proposal; he would cease to assist the Department in any further manner. Two days later the Mayor called him up to tell him that they had approved his request and he could start looking for a new evidence officer. Karen was very pleased with her new position and didn't want to do anything to mess things up. Art had a rather long sit-down with her and she came away with a very different perspective. Her perspective to this point had been that women in law enforcement had to be fairly aggressive and forceful to ever receive any respect. However, Art had now pointed out that from this point forward she needed to consider the others and not herself. This was a strange concept for Karen, but she promised him that she would do her best. As she left out he told her that he knew she would. Karen made a wonderful Assistant Chief and was even made the actual Chief four years later. The City didn't want to give her a chance at first; but Art saw what she was capable of and worked things out to where she could prove herself. He and Bill continued to help with several cases there in the City and the crime rate steadily fell.

Bill was growing old at a horrible pace, but his nose still worked as well as it ever did. *The Gray Area* used them several times each year and each time Bill showed just what he was capable of. One of their most memorable adventures was when Bill had just turned seventy years old in dog years. They were called in by Mister Frank once more and immediately took off for the airport. Over the years this same situation had happened so many times that Art and Bill were practically treated as celebrities at the airport. By the time they arrived, the people at the airport had everything ready for them and they were taken directly to their flight. They always flew first class and Art never ceased amusing himself with the reaction of the others there in first class. On one flight, one of the first class passengers refused to ride up there with a dog and requested to be moved back to the coach passenger seating. Talk about cutting your nose off to spite your face, she did. Bill let Art know that she was a cat lover and was covered in cat hair. Art continued to carry a departmental badge and as a result was allowed to carry his sidearm without question.

In the case at hand, Art and Bill were transported from the airport in Denver by a local police unit. They were taken directly to the crime scene; which turned out to be the location where the President of the United States had been delivering a speech. Not just any speech, but one to a predominantly homosexual audience. The shooter, when he fired, just missed the President and killed a very key supporter; which had been seated next to the President near the podium. The Secret Service was all over this, but had not located the shooter as of that time. By the time that Art and Bill arrived; the President was already in the air and safely out of there. The scene had been marked off just as with any other crime scene and only those with a definite need were allowed in. Quickly, the Secret Service was washing their hands of this situation and everything was falling back into the local authority's hands. It was the Secret Service that had called *The Gray Area* in to assist and that invite was fading fast as Art and Bill arrived. By this time they had discovered the location from which the shot had been fired; but no one was there and very little was left behind to further the investigation. With Art and Bill's arrival, they were hurried to the location where the shot had been fired. The Secret Service Agents weren't giving them much of a chance and told them that they needed to turn this over to the local authorities. One pass through the area and Bill fairly well knew which sent belonged to the shooter. As they left the location where the shot had actually been fired, Bill's nose was in full action and he wanted to head off in a totally separate direction from where they were being taken. Art continually pled with the officers for indulgence; as they followed Bill through the building. At one point they came up to a trash chute and Bill told Art that something had been dropped down that particular chute. This was almost at the front of the building and the officers felt that the shooter surely wouldn't have headed off towards the front of the building. With continued pleading from Art, the agents went to the area where the trash emptied out and within a few seconds had found the weapon that the shooter had used. They now knew that they were dealing with no ordinary shooter; as this rifle had been carefully crafted to resemble a walking cane. The round that this shooter fired had been built into the cane and there was no way that he could get any more than one shot.

Initially they figured that he had shot at the President and had missed; but they were definitely wrong one more time. The man that had been killed had promised to put millions into the President's reelection and all was for the direct purpose of forwarding the homosexual agenda. The shooter was well aware that you didn't kill a snake by cutting off its tail, but rather its head. It was the money that this man could use to forward this agenda that needed to be stopped; not the puppet that it put in power. Without this man's money to support this cause; this issue was dead as far as the President was concerned.

Bill continued to follow the shooter's scent and went almost up to the actual podium where the other man had died. If it hadn't been for the fact that he had been instrumental in locating the weapon; they would have already pulled the plug on this entire affair. The man's scent went all around in front of the podium and Art finally made the connection that the man had actually helped in removing the chairs from in front of the podium. In just a few minutes the Secret Service came up with the company's name, which was in charge of bringing and removing the chairs. They went to the location where the chairs had been delivered and once more Bill's nose went to work. The man they were looking for had helped unload the truck and then at one point he simply disappeared around the building. Heading down the alley next to the building, Bill came across a spot where the man had lingered. Then rather quickly he told Art that the man had left out from this location on a bicycle. Instantly the authorities were informed to stop anyone on a bike and get identification from them. It was almost seven hours later when an abandoned bike was located near a local motel. Bill by this time had followed up on no less than ten locations in the mean time, prior to his arrival at this motel. In a few seconds he told Art that the individual had used that specific bike and he even took them to the motel room that the shooter had used. Looking at the registration card, he had used a false name and had not filled in the portion that showed what type of vehicle he was driving. They checked the credit card that he had used and it was issued to a dead man. Their first lead came in checking on other charges on that same card. It seemed that there was a flight booked on that particular card in Cheyenne, Wyoming; which was a little over three hours away. By this time, that flight had taken off and had also landed in Salt Lake City, Utah. A government jet was brought to the airport and it picked Art and Bill up for a flight to Salt Lake City. When they arrived, Bill was taken to the location where the other flight had left its passengers off and he fairly quickly picked up on the man's scent once more. From there they followed that scent to a tram station and had to check every location where that tram had stopped. Finally Bill hit on one location and they followed it to a boarding area where that a flight was just leaving. They checked the flights from that boarding area and found that there had been two in the time frame that they were looking at. Art couldn't believe that the man would wait around for the second flight; so they took off for Phoenix, Arizona, where the first flight had already landed. He prayed that he had made the correct decision and upon arrival they were taken to the boarding area where the flight in question would have unloaded. Without much trouble at all Bill once again hit on the man's scent and it was even stronger than before. The more this man sweated without bathing, the stronger his scent became. He couldn't possibly know that they were on to him, but Art and Bill were in hot pursuit.

Bill followed the scent and this time it went through the main terminal area and to the road outside. This is where he lost the scent, as someone had picked the man up at this location. Just luckily it was in the cab waiting area. The agents had all of the cabs that had picked fairs up at that time return to the airport. Bill checked each one and then hit on a certain cab. By this time the agents were thinking that they were chasing a ghost, but it was all they had. The cab driver told of delivering this fair to a location on Sixth Street and how he felt uneasy; as there was no one there to meet this man. He gave a full description of the man and it fairly well matched what the flight attendants had also given them. The man was about six feet tall, dark complexion, with a small moustache, and dark medium length hair. Bill was taken to the location on Sixth Street and he instantly picked up on

the man's trail. He followed him for over five blocks
and then right up to a bus station. The man had
purchased a ticket, but under what name and to what
location they didn't know. The bus that had left out in
their time frame was headed to El Paso, Texas.
Acquiring the time log for the bus, they chose a
location and headed for the airport. If the man was still
on the bus at Gallup, New Mexico; they would be there
waiting for him. They arrived at Gallup well ahead of
the bus and were there at the bus stop when the bus
finally pulled in. Art and Bill had positioned
themselves at a point where they could be
nonchalantly standing near the bus as the passengers
walked past. The man they were looking for never
walked past that point; so they entered the bus and
walked down the aisle. At an empty seat, Bill looked at
Art and told him that the man had been seated there.
They questioned the passengers and found out that the
man in that seat had left the bus at Tucson, Arizona.
At this point the man could simply live in or near
Tucson, could have taken a second bus towards
California, or could have headed out towards Mexico.
Art looked at where all he had taken them and said
that the man was running for the border. There were
several border crossings, but only one major one near
the area where that he had exited the bus, Nogales.
With only their poor description to go by, they were
actually looking for a needle in a hay stack. To look for
a dark complected man with dark hair at the Nogales
crossing, would almost be a farce. Once more Art got
one of those gut feelings that the man would not be
driving across the border, but rather walking across.
Most of the vehicles crossing into Mexico were
videotaped for drug detection purposes and he felt that
this man would not want his picture taken. As a result
they left their main checking to the Border Patrol;

which was not accustomed to checking vehicles entering Mexico, but rather exiting. It was no time at all before they hit on a vehicle carrying several million dollars in cash money. This major find just about ended their checks on any other vehicles, as they were tied up in protecting and processing this one find. Art hoped that he had made the right decision and they stayed with the individuals walking across the border. Several times he wanted to pull off of this endeavor and head straight for the bus station at Tucson; but he couldn't continue to just follow after this ghost. They were there for almost a full day and the Secret Service Agents were ready to pull the plug on this entire endeavor. Then just as they were discussing the futility of going on; Bill hit on a group of individuals. The men were just entering the restroom and Art called for assistance. In just a few seconds, the two agents entered the restroom in search of the man that they had the wonderful description of. Art and Bill waited outside and heard nothing. Then a single man came walking out by himself and Bill definitely told Art that he was the one. The agents had not stopped him and now he was just headed for the border. However, he didn't even fit the description at all. This man was possibly six feet tall, with pale skin, no moustache, and short almost blonde hair could be seen protruding from under the edge of his baseball cap. Bill also looked at this man and knew what the problem was.

Art at this point was hesitating, as Bill almost shouted out, "Bleach, I smell bleach!"

Art knew that he had to do something quick, but just what. He pulled his pistol and shouted for the man to stop. This only caused the man to start running and now Art was really being pushed. He definitely felt compelled to do something at this point. Then without hesitating any further, he pulled his pistol up and fired a round. The large 45 round roared down the crossing and struck the man in the right buttocks. He was down, but was still desperately trying to pull himself towards the border. By this time the agents ran up and told him to stop where he was. At this point Art was seriously in trouble, if they couldn't prove that this was the man that had fired the fatal round. They took him to the local hospital and kept him under very tight surveillance. Finally the fingerprints off of the bicycle at the motel came back as being from the same man that Art had now shot. It was still an uphill battle from there, but at least Art and Bill had done their job very well. This time they actually received an accommodation from the President himself and had to go to Washington for the presentation.

Art's life had been anything but boring and he had JW to thank for most of it. He had by this time taken Bill back to his sister once more and they came clean to just who Bill truly was. When he told her of the two of them working for *The Gray Area*, she was very impressed and told them she understood. There were many fishing trips in the future for Art, Bill, Teddy, and of course Albert.

14202565R00120